SPY
within a
RUBY

Stefan A. Nicholson

Other books in this Trilogy

By Stefan Nicholson

Book One: "Spy within a Ruby"

Book Two: "Diamond for a Ruby"

Book Three: "Ruby's Covert Mission"

"The purpose of life is not just to be happy. It is also to be useful, to have honour, to be compassionate, to have made some difference for having lived . . . and lived well by helping others along the way."

~ Stefan Nicholson

SPY within a RUBY   First Edition 2018

Copyright © 2018 Stefan Andrew Nicholson, Hobart Tasmania

All rights reserved

Printed in Australia

ISBN: 978-0-9804604-9-0

Published by:

ENVIROSUPPORT

P.O. Box 370, South Hobart,

Tasmania, Australia 7004

ISBN 978-0-9804604-9-0

Website: www.stefannicholson.com

email: stefannicholson@bigpond.com   phone: +61 417 181 077

Contents

New Arrivals

It seemed to be the perfect partnership, combining a love of family life with the erratic necessities of running a business.

Mum ran the 'Mayfair Mews' hotel with a friendly southern air of self-importance whilst Dad did most of the maintenance in the off-season when he was not driving his own taxi. Dad's Yorkshire upbringing was the leveller for any misconceptions about what a business was and what could easily be an expensive hobby.

There were sixteen individual suites set out in a landscaped garden overlooking a fountain.

They did have a son too, called Eric.

Oh, Eric was useful for doing the odd job now and again alright but at sixteen years old, well he was battling his final year at school whilst trying to woo his childhood sweetheart who lived down the road. She hated him. Ruby hated everybody.

And so, the Johnson's now eagerly awaited their guests with their freshly painted and re-carpeted hotel oozing charm and quality - for the summer holidays had arrived.

There was nothing to indicate that this year was going to be any different than the previous ten years which had passed quite smoothly except for the flooding, wind damage and . . . that unfortunate death of an American visitor.

He did say that he felt 'a bit off'.

"I'm going to pick up that Chinese lady from the airport Milly," shouted Dad through the servery hatch to Mum "I'll be about an hour."

Mum was getting used to be called Milly even by guests these days instead of the more formal Millicent that her parents still used when talking down to her. Robert Angus Johnson or Robbie to family and friends and her husband of eighteen years, used to introduce her as a 'tenner', the one thousand cent wonder. Well, it was better than the initial millipede jibe – the one with the thousand shoes. Milly loved her shoes!

"Ok Robbie," replied Mum excitedly "I'll get Eric to help me prepare the salads and dessert."

Robbie raised his eyebrows and sighed.

"Good luck with that one!"

Eric was often credited with having super-human hearing or even the ability to predict the first flicker of a thought about any impending work in the minds of his parents. The back door squeaked closed behind him.

Robbie drove his three-year-old black Lexus to the airport, passing by the Defence Research Industry plant which had only just been built. No one knew what they did there, but many locals imagined it was a place where military personnel went to retire.

They called it the DRIP. There was a lot of active security going on with vehicles, helicopters and military personnel carrying automatic weapons, perhaps indicating that they didn't want to be disturbed.

Robbie had timed his arrival at the airport just right to suit the landing of the plane as well as the usual ten-minute delay waiting at the baggage area.

Sure enough, walking towards him with suitcase in hand was a Chinese lady with trench coat and sunglasses. And another one!

Robbie grabbed the first woman and confirmed that she was indeed his fare. Many a competitor would 'steal' passengers with the guise of being unable to understand them – at first.

Angie the female cabbie from the larger town of Doulton was next in line for picking up passengers and ran up to the other Chinese lady who had a baby in a stroller. Angie had been a cabbie for a few years, arriving from Scotland with her husband Angus who was an engineer. She loved to mess about with customers in a friendly manner and make them feel at ease and make them laugh. It usually worked a treat.

"You have woom for baby please?" asked the lady politely.

"Yes, I have a womb but it is full . . . prior commitment. Ha Ha . . . You can't put them back you know," she quipped.

The lady looked unsure at first, before laughing and pointing at Angie's baby bump.

Robbie was laughing to himself before turning towards his fare, a now frosty looking proposition with raised sunglasses and a piercing stare. He nearly fell over backwards.

"I hope you are a more civilised example of what England has to offer a woman of my credentials," she snapped, pushing her suitcase into his knee.

"Oh, she's not from here love, she is from that tribe to the north of us, pure Scot with a love of life. She means well and was only being friendly," replied Robbie.

It was a long silent trip home until the lady saw the Mayfair Mews property in all its glory. She looked at Robbie kindly.

"Thank you. I am so sorry I was very short with you but I have had no proper sleep for two days," she said sheepishly, "I will feel better tomorrow."

Robbie nodded and smiled at her, then proceeded to remove her luggage from the boot. He felt that the explanation was quite valid.

A small white van across the road caught his eye. It looked like a telecom van which made him feel quite apprehensive, having just spent the last six weeks sorting out their Internet booking system problems. The driver was sitting at the wheel resting his head against the window.

"Typical," he thought, shaking his head "another rort on the taxpayers."

The driver was watching him out of the corner of his eye. He scribbled down a note and mumbled into his lapel microphone. The camera on the side-mirror made a series of quick snaps and then almost immediately the engine was started.

"Proceed to the writer's dinner Davis and get some info on the guests and that St John Smythe chap. He has come under a cloud recently regarding leaked documents and we think he'll be meeting prospective buyers there this afternoon," directed the voice through his earpiece.

Roger Davis drove off slowly, thinking about the undercover disguise he would use for the dinner.

He needed to invent an abstract, non-famous, socially irritating character with which to meet as many people as possible to find out their basic profile, before they could utterly despise him and run away. He always tried to have some fun before things turned nasty . . . and they usually did, with dire consequences.

Robbie closed the boot of his car loudly to signal that a guest had arrived.

As usual, Mum nonchalantly flowed out from the front door of the hotel to greet her guest.

"Madame Jin?"

"Yes, Jin Shi Tian . . . hello, you have a beautiful place. Please just call me Tian."

"And I am Milly . . . and you have met my husband Robert, or Robbie as we call him. Welcome to the Mayfair Mews and I hope you will enjoy your stay with us. I will show you to your suite so you can get settled first . . . then we have tea starting from three thirty in the dining room until five o'clock . . . or you may have your meal sent up to your suite. Dinner is from six thirty till nine thirty. We have a superb chef who can make anything that you desire."

Tian was most impressed with the delightful service so far.

"But he can't make desserts like our Milly," added Robbie.

Tian nodded her head as Milly gave her the security tab for her suite. It was number six, ideal for the use of a Chinese guest as it supposedly has some lucky connotation.

Milly started her urgent up-market history of the area, especially concerning the unfortunate village name of Dogbol.

"The village name is of course pronounced 'Dodge Bull', referring to an heroic royal figure who dived in front of a wild bull to save the life of a poor local child many centuries ago."

Robbie was shaking his head, which caught Tian's attention.

He put his hands to his head to make two ears and whispered "Woof, Woof," behind Milly's back.

Tian's broad smile was worth the effort. Milly turned around.

Luckily the phone rang just as Robbie was quickly picking up Tian's two suitcases. He ran to the reception counter, picked up the phone and nervously rummaged through the in-tray for any new arrival information. There was just the one letter there and he read it as he answered the call.

"Good afternoon, Mayfair Mews, Robbie speaking."

Out of the corner of his eye, he caught the shadowy outline of his son, slinking by way of the bar to the back entrance of the kitchen.

"There goes another dent in our expenses," he mumbled, shaking his head and dumping the unrelated letter back into the in-tray.

"Hello, hello, is that the Mayfair Hotel," issued the deep gruff voice on the phone.

He sounded like a Russian or had some sort of Slavic accent.

"Yes, hello there, you have the Mayfair Mews. I am the manager, Robbie Johnson . . . and how may I help you?"

"Mews? Mews? What is this mews?"

"Well, apart from the repetitive sound coming out of our cantankerous cat . . . this mews is an hotel sir. It is a quaint old Englishy thing I'm afraid . . . I'm sure 'hotel' would have sufficed for most normal people, but apparently not for my dear southern wife," replied Robbie with a bit of a laugh.

There was a moment of silence with each one wondering whose turn it was to speak.

"So, can I help you with some accommodation or perhaps a booking for dinner tonight in our splendid restaurant . . . the famous 'Prince and Bull'?"

"I just require accommodation and no bull," he replied mildly amused and hiding his desire to laugh.

"Where did she put the reservation?" murmured Robbie to himself, not listening fully to the caller as he searched under the in-tray and desktop for any trace of this guest. But he could not find even a scribbled note.

"May I have your name then sir, so that I can check you off our reservation?"

"Chuck me off reservation? I am not native American Indian Robbie! Ha Ha. We Russians do have sense of humour."

"Yes quite, that was very witty I must say . . . and your name please?"

"Ilya Kasparov . . . and no, I do not have a booking . . . this is why I am phoning you now, but don't worry, I will not be arriving at hotel until tomorrow."

"Oh, I see then, right . . . so you're not Russian right over then, so to speak. Well, you are in luck because we do have a suite available for you. How long will you be staying with us?"

"Four weeks should be long enough to do my work . . . I am visiting lecturer in Mathematics at your university. Good, good . . . I have your email from web page so that I will send all my details to you before I arrive."

Robbie was getting very excited at the prospect of having another long-term guest.

Tian the Chinese lady was also staying for three to four weeks depending on how her business convention plans panned out.

Robbie scribbled down the details on the reservation note pad for Milly to follow up and enter into the computer.

"Thank you Mr Kasparov, I have made the reservation and will return-email your suite details along with the hotel invoice and payment methods. Is there anything else I can help you with?"

"No, thank you. I send email soon and look forward to see you at your cat hotel. Ha Ha."

"Thank you and I look forward to seeing you too. Goodbye," replied Robbie laughing unconvincingly, before shaking his head, mumbling, "and I'll make sure there's a bowl of warm milk available on your arrival."

Milly had returned from showing Tian her suite and was staring at him from the foyer.

"It will drop off one day!"

"What?" queried Robbie angrily.

"Your head . . . you are always shaking your head and tut tutting all my comments when I try to raise the standard of this place. You think everything is so funny . . . or awkwardly irritating."

Robbie thought about whether to reply or just keep busy.

"You could make an effort to promote the history of our village and its ancestral heritage to the throne of England," continued Milly.

Robbie imagined a set of corgis eating their dinner off gold monogrammed plates.

"You need a modern approach to marketing Milly. Quite frankly the story about the village name is a lot of bull. Even the local kids call it Dog Bowl. Why we had to have a Mews instead of a Bark is beyond me."

"Now you're being really silly."

"Well, I am now a local," he murmured.

Robbie thought for a while.

"At least we have some up-market, professional clientele these days and I wouldn't think that they are interested in folk-lore voodoo . . . waffle about medieval Jersey Cows."

Milly ignored him as usual and headed for the kitchen. Eric was coming the other way shielding what looked like a steak sandwich and a pile of chips.

Robbie shook his head and sighed loudly, "Ah, our official medieval food taster has arrived."

It was an off-day for Robbie who could be most charming and thoughtful when he was not responsible for anything to do with trivial tasks.

Taxi driving was the perfect job for him - short term interaction with customers and working when he wanted to.

To the trained eye, there always seemed to be some sort of apprehension or longing for earlier days in his quiet moments, especially when talking to Ruby's father, the equally private Harry Peters.

Harry had something to do with bulk transport - trucks, boats and air-freight – with an office in outer London and another office in the port of Liverpool.

Harry and Robbie would always attend an annual gathering in Scotland and the occasional meet-up in London with their friends. They said it was a gathering of mates for lake fishing and running their fishing club.

Milly dreaded these trips away. He always came back most unsettled and usually half hung-over.

Orfur Convention

The balmy summer afternoon was coming to a close as seen by the longer shadows stretching out over the marquee long-tables at the Writer's Convention. This year it was being held at pompous Lord Rupert Pertwee's sprawling estate located about one mile from the Mayfair Mews hotel.

A certain James Bartholomew Watt, alias Roger Davis – MI6 operative was pressed up against one of the food tables, armed with two plates. One hand had two fingers wrapped around a champagne glass, whilst clutching a plate of Atlantic salmon with his remaining fingers.

The other hand occasionally put down the loaded plate of party pies and quiche tarts in order to eat. There were crumbs and pastry flakes scattered all around his old weathered boots.

He looked a scruffy, ruffled sort of fellow with wild hair and an oversized white jacket covering up a blue shirt and brown baggy trousers. He enjoyed a good undercover assignment.

He certainly contrasted with the other writers who were trying to impress each other with vague phrases and quotes from obscure books and who wore smart casual or smart very casual outwardly-labelled clothes. Well, they were writers imitating what they thought successful writers should wear and say.

Watt looked as though he was only there for the food, but an observant crime writer would immediately recognise that there was an alternative reason for his apparent eccentricity and fool's play.

Now Lord Pertwee was no crime writer or close to being an intellectual, but he did like a good mystery or two with a criminal bent. He did not take too kindly to what he thought was a gate-crashing vagrant.

"And what have we here then . . . eh? So why are you attending this international gala dinner for famous authors . . . hmmmm?" he asked sarcastically.

"Oim an orfur mister . . . dat is what I am sir . . . an orfur of some note," replied Davis enthusiastically.

"Pardon? An awful what?"

"An orfur sir is what I be . . . an orfur of books. An orfur lot of books."

"Oh, I see . . . an author. Well then, and may I enquire, what genre do you write in . . . do you do your orfuring in then?"

"No . . . no I don't do no John Arr or any other orfur . . . cos I don't do dem homdilooms. I write dem books in me own name sir . . . bein' an orfur," replied Davis.

Lord Pertwee was beside himself.

"What?"

"See now, you must have read one of me books den seein' as you know me name an all that," quipped Davis, nudging him sharply in the arm.

"What books?"

"Dem are the ones sir. Exactly . . . writed up by me . . . James Bartholomew Watt," pointed out Davis, tipping an imaginary hat.

"He invented the steam engine . . . if I'm not mistaken?" said Lord Pertwee, now getting angry.

"No . . . no that wun is not from me. Oi didn't orfur dat wun.
No . . . I don't think so . . . not dem steam engines . . . no."

Lord Pertwee was getting very annoyed and looked Davis
directly in the eye, grabbing him firmly by the collar.

"Now look here you . . . you scoundrel. That's a nice try but
you can't just sneak in here and help yourself to free food with
a tale like that."

Davis gave him a wink and came closer to his ear.

"Exactly I'm sure sir. No sneakin' around while I'm orfuring .
. . no sir. Not while I'm orfurring books for a living . . . as an
orfur."

Lord Pertwee was fuming. This man was having a lend of him.

"I'm going to call security in 5 seconds if you don't . . ."

Davis realised that he had played around a bit too much.

"Oim jus goin to say one word."

"What?"

Davis looked at him and muttered his saving grace.

"No sir . . . that wasn't it. I was goin' to say . . . publisher . . .
that was it sir."

Lord Pertwee with hands on hips, rocked back a little in
disbelief at the new change in direction for this 'orfur'. Some of
the convention writers had gathered around. Now was not the
time to seem ruthless. He decided to play along.

"Publisher! Oh, of course you didn't fool me for a moment. I
thought that this man . . . is not an orfur . . . no, not an orfur
but a bloody famous publisher who publishes books for those
other unemployed orfurs . . . authors."

Davis looked relieved.

"You have dat completely right sir . . . you have met yourself a publisher who helps orfurs to make dem books of theirs so that ordinary folk can read dem fine books after some adjustin and shoving and pushing around the dribble until they are published proper like. The only orfurring that I be doing now is dat orferring of books for sale . . . on behalf of orfurs and the other half which is . . . me, meself sir."

Lord Pertwee looked around him and continued his sarcastic and aloof tirade, playing up to some of the others gathered around in amusement.

"I see it all now . . . of course . . . how could I miss your exemplary use of the English language and an obvious passion for the business of orfurring."

"And publishing," added Davis quickly.

"So I suppose you have a premises . . . an office suite or dare I say a building in the city where you are located for such work wiv orfurs?" asked Lord Pertwee sarcastically.

"Indeed yes sir . . . in dat high street dere and up the lonely little lane that is home to struggling orfurs . . . where they come for the attention of a humble publisher . . . the likes of me self."

Lord Pertwee thought about his town layout.

"And exactly how far . . . up the lane do you have to go then?"

"There's a big sign up there to show the way for them orfurs to find . . . on dere way to get from orfurring to publishing all in the best part of a half hour," replied Davis with authority.

"What big sign?"

"Ah . . . you are not an orfur den sir? Ah well, it can look like a giant red cat to some folk . . . but to night travellers, who have rested up there orfurring . . . it can look like a ferocious red dragon . . . spitting out fire and . . ."

Lord Pertwee cut him off.

"Are we talking about the Red Lion Pub then . . . where lazy, scruffy, idle people drink away the hours of the day and night . . . and . . ."

"Ah dat'll be dem no good orfurs with no money and no use of a publisher," interrupted an apparently annoyed Davis.

Lord Pertwee rubbed his chin and rocked on his heels like the stereotypical beat cop.

"To recap then. You publish from inside the Red Lion Pub on the high street and . . ."

Davis interrupted.

"Most of the time sir . . . most of the time I publish inside dat fine house . . . unless I'm publishing outside on de pavement when there's a crisis . . . and I find myself cast out . . . of the publishing process . . . by a wild orfur possessed by greed and some Guinness sir."

Lord Pertwee sighed with despair. The gathered crowd had dispersed in order to promote themselves more to anyone who looked remotely interested . . . or even not interested at all.

After looking around for some sort of exit strategy he spied an old rival, an elite like himself, Lord Jeremy St John Smythe, who was even snootier than himself.

Quick thinking Lord Pertwee waved to Jeremy to come over.

"Ah Jeremy . . . long time between our pathways crossing, eh?"

"Quite Pertwee old man. Still getting a free feed . . . what?"

"Oh quite. How droll. Anyway, I'd like you to meet a good friend of mine."

Lord Pertwee moved closer to Jeremy and whispered, "He's an actor in disguise to go along with the gala dinner. He mingles with guests to add some authenticity to what these orfurs . . . I mean authors do whilst writing."

Jeremy was impressed.

"What a clever idea old man. Who is he then?"

"Mum's the word old chap . . . top international actor . . . in disguise of course . . . we'll call him Watt."

"What?" asked Jeremy.

"Yes, Watt. That's his name. James Watt."

"Didn't he invent . . .?"

"No, no . . . that was his uncle's cousin, I think. I'll introduce you. Mr Watt, this is Lord Jeremy St John Smythe . . . and this is a James Bartholomew Watt."

Jeremy eyed up the dishevelled Davis and winced.

"How do you do old chap. Mum's the word. Let me get you another glass of champagne."

Davis stood in front of Lord Jeremy and snapped his photo on a lapel camera.

"Hello then guvnor . . . yes I'm an orfur . . . an orfur of dem books . . . and publish inside and outside of me premises in de high street there."

Jeremy was still both fascinated and amused at this novel approach to liven up a typically boring writer's convention.

"An orfur my words . . . and a publisher to boot. I'll show you around and introduce you to some of the people . . . in your disguise of course. See if you can fool them, eh Watt . . . what?"

Lord Pertwee gave Davis a pat on the back and walked away at a quick pace and with a broad smile.

Davis the operative in the guise of James Bartholomew Watt had successfully made contact with his first mark – Jeremy St John Smythe, the well-connected director at the new Defence Research Industry plant.

"I may orfur up a little book about this very day Guvnor . . . and publish it me self as an Orfur of dem finest of words. . . then orfur them books for sale . . . an orfur lot of dem books too. Orfur the sake of makin' a humble living. As they say you know . . . orfur one and orfur all!"

"I say, you are a bit of a ham aren't you Watt . . . what?"

They both laughed as Jeremy guided Davis slowly around the convention, spoofing it up with his acting, whilst getting introduced to all the foreign writers – asking about their work and covertly taking their photos.

Davis noticed two individuals who were constantly in the shadowy background, both pretending to be enjoying the conversation of others . . . and yet appeared to be anticipating a brief word with Lord Jeremy. They didn't however speak to each other, which was even more interesting.

He could see and hear that the calm vibrant lady was mainland Chinese but it was hard to pin down the accent of the tall thick-framed man with the deep quiet voice. He looked more and more agitated.

Years of experience told him that the man was a Russian or at least he grew up there. A quick message back from his earpiece confirmed the identities of both suspects based on the photos he had sent but not only that . . . the false names they had used to enter the country was also important to him.

"Jin Shi Tian and Ilya Kasparov eh . . . quite the heavy negotiators," he mumbled to himself.

He now knew that they were both booked into the Mayfair Mews hotel officially but they obviously had more secretive options for their work - maybe at the home of Jeremy St John Smythe or one of his close friends.

Davis was distracted momentarily by some of the party guests.

The delegates were now quite lively and boisterous from the effects of the champagne and he played up to them staying in character.

"Hey Mr Watt, can we have a picture taken with you for our friends to see? It's not often we meet a real 'orfur' you know."

"Of course, yes, I'll give you a few hints on how to shove and push and choose your words carefully before you get whacked by the editor. It's always to the head you know," replied Davis dryly, trying to concentrate on the goings on.

The Chinese lady was quick to swoop in to have a brief and what looked like a stern few words with Jeremy who appeared quite nonchalant. She cut a fine figure with an interesting face.

"Much higher," gestured the aloof Jeremy, tapping his nose.

Tian looked around to see his minder moving closer and the large frame of Kasparov coming over to see them. Tian moved away quickly, smiling at Kasparov.

"Ah, Ilya my good friend . . . have you had any luck with getting the resources to purchase the rights to my forthcoming work?" asked Jeremy with a broad smile.

"Lord Jeremy, it is not what I planned, to see you here in such a public place . . . but I can see your concerns . . . for your ability to keep on producing such high-quality manuscripts."

"Only the best will do . . . for us both Ilya, you know that much at least. The competition is always trying to bump me off the best seller list," said Jeremy coldly.

Kasparov looked in the direction that Tian was headed.

"I have a million reasons for avoiding a trip to China to recover such a work should it end up in their book club. That is all I have. Interesting . . . yes?"

"Interesting but early days yet Ilya. I think at this stage there are more avid readers," replied Jeremy again touching his nose.

Kasparov looked around him quickly, then into Jeremy's eyes, sensing the approaching minder. He pushed a package into Jeremy's hand.

"There will be no more offer . . . maybe no one will want what is yesterday's news my friend. Enjoy your present."

Jeremy held the present up to his nose and put it into his inside pocket.

Davis arrived just in time to see Kasparov leaving, checking over his shoulder to acknowledge that indeed a certain Mr Watt was not so much undercover.

"Roger Davis," whispered Kasparov to himself with a smirk.

At the back of his mind Davis was working on a new plan for when the 'orfurring' charade was over. After all, he was the top operative of MI6 sent undercover to investigate the leaking of information at the Defence Research Industry plant.

He wondered whether to continue his play-acting but now as the undercover persona, 'Professor Roland the academic' for the entire stay albeit toned down, in order to be taken seriously as a seconded lecturer and not an absolute moron.

However, now that he had been recognised by Kasparov and more than likely by Jin Shi Tian and Jeremy, there was no further need for such eccentricity. He lamented that the fun was indeed over.

His communicator indicated that there was a waiting message. After playing it back, the object of interest for Davis turned to be the Mayfair Mews hotel, the official accommodation for the two persons of interest because it was so close to the plant.

Davis dropped his 'Watt' impersonation and excused himself in his 'normal, false street voice' from the company of Lord Jeremy. It was a light Irish accent with a polite firmness to match the occasion.

"Lord Jeremy I'd like to thank you for putting up with my antics this afternoon and I have very much enjoyed talking with you, but now I must go to another appointment."

"Well done old chap, well done for adding some life to this narcissistic woodpeckering by all and sundry, all eager to gain the last morsel of attention from anyone willing to listen."

They shook hands and smiled. Lord Jeremy looked a bit edgy as if he already knew more than he should. Davis could see more.

"It's the details that give things away in the end . . . if you're observant enough or willing to see," replied Davis dryly.

"Yes, it is often an act of mercy to destroy a fake too," murmured Jeremy to Davis, raising his eyebrows.

"There's many a fake hanging in the houses of the rich," replied Davis, touching and stretching his neck.

Lord Jeremy half-smiled and took a closer look at this master of disguise. As Davis turned to leave, Jeremy rubbed his nose with his middle finger, attracting the gaze of his minder. He then nodded for him to take a much closer interest in this man.

Davis checked his message – 'Media PR briefing at plant 1500hrs tomorrow'. It was now six thirty in the evening, leaving plenty of time to stake out where Lord Jeremy was headed and with whom he was meeting.

King's Club

The afternoon was coming to an end, evidenced by the cooler air and dark shadows stretching out over the now messy, wind-blown marquee tables at the Writer's Convention.

Cleaning staff were already clearing empty tables and all those nooks and crannies where party people love to congregate, to whisper tantalising tales of lies and deception in order to gain favour or to con anyone into reading their manuscripts.

'Rich and famous' certainly beats 'poor and unfashionable' any day. This was the playground for innuendo, smart biting comments, terrible jokes and downright trashy behaviour.

Lord Pertwee was surveying the closing moments of the latest public invasion to his family estate from the lower wing windows, thankful that the revenue may well help to pay for the restoration of his favourite reception room and thus opening up the house for more tourists.

He avoided looking at the portrait of his late grandfather who always seemed to mock him for getting into such financial strife.

Lord Jeremy's silver 'Roller' pulled up alongside him and a splendidly stereotypical chauffeur with a face so deadpan that it may have previously belonged to a corpse, got out of the car and opened the rear right-hand door.

"Take me to my club Wilkins," said Lord Jeremy without looking at him, "and pick me up at ten o'clock sharp."

He eased back into the plush leather seat and reached for his newly acquired cigar, pushed into his hand by the Russian, Kasparov.

In fact, what makes the 'Gurkha His Majesties Reserve' so special is that its eighteen-year-old tobacco leaves are soaked in 'Louis XIII de Rémy Martin' cognac, itself the most rare and expensive cognac in the world. Each box of twenty cigars soaked in one whole bottle of these two thousand five hundred dollar-a-bottle cognac costs fifteen thousand dollars.

Sure, it was no ordinary cigar at seven hundred and fifty dollars each, but then these were no ordinary times and there was a promise of more such cigars should everything go alright with the handover of the complete backup of the 'AI Soldier' project action files.

A phone call broke through the lazy day-dreaming mind of Jeremy into the need to maintain security. The privacy screen was activated and closed fully before Jeremy reached for the phone.

"Yes, Sir Rodney . . . yes, I'm on my way now. There in ten minutes and I must say these cigars are something to die for."

There was obviously a witty reply back.

"Well, of course I don't mean us old chap but those expendable geeks at the M.O.D. and maybe an occasional Russian or Chinese tourist," laughed Lord Jeremy, "Oh, and there's a PR circus at the plant tomorrow. I'll send Cartwright with his scanning gear to distance myself from all the publicity and all, although I will be there officially as a director. Yes, see you soon."

It was getting dark and it looked like it would rain. The 'Roller' moved quietly and smoothly through the city streets as Jeremy watched the 'ordinary' folk trudging around doing last minute shopping, shuffling home weary from mundane work or as he often thought, beckoning death to take them during the short resting part of their monotonous, captive, humiliating survival-cycle, prior to the much-welcomed tranquiliser period, sometimes called sleep.

The entrance to the 'King's Club' was old and shabby but retained that grandiose facade from three hundred years of private goings-on, where deals were made, people elevated way beyond their means or entitlements were 'granted'.

Some were politicians and even previous prime ministers and some were just international scoundrels who could pay their way to acquiring more power and wealth than can be imagined.

Lord Jeremy was greeted at the front door and with a few nods to various regulars he made his way to the back room. The door was manned by another club official, a much bigger individual with his right hand inside his inner jacket and most alert to anyone or anything that crossed his path.

"They say I may enjoy a cigar or two here?" asked Lord Jeremy to the guard at the door.

The guard nodded and pressed the electronic unlocking device to open the steel door still looking ahead at the front entrance foyer.

Lord Jeremy entered the luxuriously decorated room and walked up to his reserved chair as everyone watched without speaking.

He sat down, reached for his glass of whisky. Showing the glass to all around, he turned to the portrait of Rupert Winston and gave his expected 'entrance toast'.

"Here is to Rupert Winston and my fellow colleagues of the 'Cigar Club'. May we honour our values and value our honours."

"Bravo, welcome old chap," said Sir Rodney who was the current head of this very private club within a club.

The other four attendees all welcomed Lord Jeremy as they waited to come to order by Sir Rodney.

"Gentlemen I'll be brief and allow Cartwright to prepare for a media PR event tomorrow at the plant. Jeremy will be present in his role as director with the officials and their military guests. He has informed me that we have at least two potential buyers for the planned access to defence military secrets - with some of our Arab partners willing to pay up front . . . but, well we do have some concerns regarding our welfare. The winning party or losing party may want to eliminate all of us to cover the leak.

We do have our weaknesses – family, business, money, property - all accessible these days to anyone with determination."

Everyone nodded and mumbled in agreement.

"There's also MI6 of course snooping around. A Roger Davis was at the Writing Convention today disguised as a writer and observed that I have been contacted by Ilya Kasparov and Jin Shi Tian," interrupted Lord Jeremy.

"How do you disguise yourself as a writer for heaven's sake?" asked Roland Campignon dryly.

Everyone smirked and waited for someone to answer.

"Well, it's more what they say than how they look Roland. All those that I spoke to had a common theme of appearing quite desperate and talked about themselves the whole time. They would do just about anything to see their names and photoshopped PR photos in the public domain as an author," answered Lord Jeremy tersely.

"Quite. Now first off then, this 'Artificial Intelligence Soldier' project that we talked about last time appears to be a long-term drawn-out process. Apparently, everyone's doing it and I'm not willing to stick my neck out for something that will be hard to sell and is somewhat dangerous to handle.

In fact, apart from having AI control and reasoning from the private encoded cloud computing portals, it seems that the structure of these humanoid type creatures is also augmented by restructured DNA to make them fearless, feel no pain and have no moral ethics at all or any limits for their reason to kill nominated targets. They may also have artificial limbs and shielding instead of the original flesh," continued Sir Rodney.

"So how on earth would we sell them without the userware commands for what our client's require of them?" asked Lord Roxburgh.

There was a buzzing of ideas until Sir Rodney brought them to order again.

"Our original mission was to obtain the complete plans for this project including the details on how to control and use these androids . . . and capture . . . and capture at least two of them for our buyers," said Sir Rodney with an air of sheer folly.

"Just a walk in the park before you realise it's an open wildlife game park and we're the antelope," joked Lord Jeremy quietly to Roland Campignon.

"It sounds too dangerous to me," interrupted Roland.

"They are really, in effect similar to normally functioning humans with a built-in hypnotic sleeper command centre so I'm told. This method has been used for years by the Russians and Americans to get ordinary people to assassinate others without them being fully aware of what they are doing.

They may get a phone call or someone might say a key phrase to them . . . and they are off on a wild killing frenzy. They know nothing about it once the deed is done and so can pass lie detector tests and interrogations without implicating anyone. They are deemed to be aggressively hostile at best," replied a worried Lord Jeremy.

There was a silence as they all thought about such a whimsical and dangerous idea until Sir Rodney eased their fears.

"Gentlemen, gentlemen you may be relieved to know that I have decided that it is too risky and problematical, apart from the dangers of playing with the human mind . . . and quite incredibly . . . another more lucrative project has come to my attention. It is called the MEEB project."

"Good heavens what is a MEEB?" asked Roland lazily.

Everyone else just stared blankly at Sir Rodney and then at each other, some shaking their heads in disbelief that this project actually sounded stupid before it had been explained.

Sir Rodney pulled down the white board which was completely filled with just one simple illustration.

"See here now, this is the MEEB project. A real game-changer in the art of modern warfare as it completely negates the capacity of the huge investment in armament, ships, planes, communications, missiles, nuclear weapons and tanks made by most developed countries and is completely invisible to the naked eye. And it is British!"

"Hoorah!" shouted an excited Lord Roxburgh without thinking.

"So why do we want to sell it to other countries?" asked Jeremy slyly.

"To make money of course . . . and to ensure that it never, ever works," whispered Sir Rodney raising his eyebrows. "We are not traitors. We are in fact sovereign patriots who finance and reward ourselves for our efforts in keeping our enemies dumb."

Everyone stared at the illustration. It looked like a group of spheres under the water . . . and under the land! The expanded title confirmed their wildest imagination as to what it was.

"Gentlemen, this is the 'Magma Entry Electro-Magnetic Bomb' or MEEB," ushered Sir Rodney.

"Looks like the spheres roam the magma and get pushed into volcanic vents and the like. I presume that they detonate and knock out all electronic devices . . . quite amazing and undetectable. Invasion from below the Earth's surface!" offered Roland, the scientific expert in the group.

"We don't have to know how it works, why it works or where they will be built because we are only interested in selling the information . . . albeit much altered to make them duds. We don't want these nasties plaguing the world. Things can get out of hand very quickly," continued Sir Rodney rolling up the white board and tidying his table-top.

Everyone else started gathering up their few belongings and waited for the official wind-up of their strange meeting. There was a tapping on the table – three solid knocks as usual.

"We will gather again gentlemen to continue our quest and we will depart now with our club motto and ethos. If you will please charge your glasses," said Sir Rodney raising his glass to arm's length.

They all chanted the same ritual toast, as always gazing at the portrait of their founder, Rupert Winston.

"We take no sides, yet serve near and far

To protect England's shores, we raise our hats.

Our risk is clear but **C. I G A. R**.

We care nought about fear saying **C**ould **I G**ive **a R**ats."

They all sculled their drinks, shouted 'Hurrah!' and slammed the glasses down on the table before getting up and walking out without another word spoken between them.

Sitting in the lounge near the foyer, a relaxed Roger Davis was reading a newspaper and ironically smoking a cigar.

As the 'Cigar Club' members left the 'King's Club', Davis was verifying the identity of each of them, mulling over the part that each one might play in their dealings with the foreign spies and with Lord Jeremy's senior position at the Defence Research Industry plant.

Village Folk

The next morning, Milly set out from the Mayfair Mews heading for a ten o'clock appointment at the hairdressers. She liked to support local businesses and was on the committee for encouraging more people to visit Dogbol and even move there.

It was such a lovely day that she decided to catch the bus for a change. It was always nice to be a passenger in Robbie's taxi but it was the busy season and he was generally booked up.

The hidden factor in her decision to catch public transport was that as a result of an argument with Robbie the night before, Milly was out to prove for herself that the local people were not country yokels. Not all of them anyway.

Robbie had called her a 'daft cat' to reason, telling her that the medieval village idiot must have acted like a human rabbit.

There were one or two strange people around who had obviously swayed Robbie's views . . . and he did remove some of the children from lying on the road outside the hotel.

They said that they were testing the hypothesis that most people would stop, as part of their school project!

Milly wondered if Robbie would stop, now that they had given him a piece of their mind, mainly the rudest part and called him a 'tacky' driver.

As she was imagining visiting Robbie in jail, the number sixteen bus arrived on time at the stop right outside their hotel. There were quite a few people on board this inter-town commuter including some children. The driver seemed to be a very friendly woman.

She had a light Liverpool accent and an infectious, if not permanent smile. Milly thought it was probably a good line of defence against dealing with the public.

There was an empty seat just behind the middle opening doors. Milly sat down and looked out of the window at the shining facade and manicured grounds of her hotel just as a portly man in a suit dashed to the front door of the bus. He waived his pass at the ticket machine and walked down the aisle towards a seat on her right.

A nervous scruffy mischievous little man occupied the space of two seats. He had a wild beard and bushy moustache that looked as though they were stuck on. Milly observed that he may even be quite young but she didn't want to stare.

"Excuse me . . . could you move over a little so that I may sit down, please . . . if you could, please?" said the portly man to the bearded man in a posh accent.

"Why don't you sit down there, next to that fat tramp?" replied the bearded man in a gruff voice, yet a little high in tone.

"Are you talking to me there? How dare you . . . I'm a Bank Manager; I'll have you know."

"Why no, I wasn't talking to you . . . I was talking about you . . . round about you . . . you are very round," replied the rude bearded man.

"I shall ignore you sir for you are not worth bothering about," replied the angry Bank Manager.

"Just like your customers I presume, you pompous, fat pen pusher."

The Bank Manager lifted up his newspaper to cover his face and muttered to himself.

"Obviously another whacko with a deranged mind and no mortgage to speak about."

"Well. . . I am still waiting to sit down! I will not be distracted by your coarse interpretations of life or by your lack of manners sir," shouted the portly man still waiting to sit down.

"Oh, quite right old bean . . . I mean you did acquire status by your old lady clawing up the ranks of the empire, eh!"

"You are a rude, deranged, obnoxious little cretin . . . but I demand my seat. Our family always gets their seat in the end you know," replied the man, looking around for praise.

One lady near the front clapped before looking embarrassed.

Milly kept her gaze out of the window and let her thoughts drift away from the situation developing on the bus.

"Move along down there. Please sit down before I drive off," shouted the driver pleasantly and probably still smiling.

"I can see that you are biased and by that, I mean you have an arse twice as big as anyone else's – probably from sitting on your seat in a boring office or at a private club bar at the expense of everyone on this bus. This seat is taken but if you insist then you shall have it," said the obnoxious, little bearded man.

And with that, he mischievously got out a custard pie and squashed it into the seat next to him.

"Move along down there," shouted the happy driver again.

The portly man moved to sit next to Milly. It was a bit of a squeeze but Milly could sense that he was not in the mood for a courtesy greeting.

She decided never to catch the bus again. The bus remained very quiet except for the obnoxious little man's humming and talking to himself in various excruciatingly irritating voices – and answering himself back.

Unknown to Milly, some children were filming their in-situ comedy documentary, completely without the passenger's permission of course – for another school project.

Milly got off two stops before she should after battling to get out of her seat and briskly walked the remaining distance to the hairdressers where she was warmly welcomed.

"Hello Milly, take a seat love and I'll be with you in five minutes," said Irene the shop's owner.

Milly began to calm down and passed off the bus episode as just a silly isolated incident . . . another one! She cursed Robbie again.

Irene was in her late forties and was a drawcard for women wanting to have a general natter and a cup of tea whilst having minor changes done to their hair. Today there were two other women gossiping amongst themselves.

Mabel and Sally were known to have the most unusual conversations, mainly attributable to early-stage dementia. They lived at the retirement home on the outskirts of town where they would plan daily trips to the pub, the library and the hairdressers.

Irene would let them sit in her salon for about an hour if it wasn't busy before moving them along with the enticement of a free gift if they would come back on a Tuesday.

They never remembered the offer by the end of the day and would instantly arrive the very next day at exactly ten o'clock.

Milly sat down next to Sally who gave her a vague smile before resuming her conversation with Mabel. Her eyes seemed to wander from being cross-eyed to being out of focus.

"My Aunty has a big lump on her face," said Mabel out of the blue.

"Is it cancer?" replied Sally totally disinterested.

"No, it's her nose and it is so big now that they had to do biopsies – you know sticking needles in and removing bits for seeing what's wrong."

"Oh, that poor woman."

"Yes, it's a shame . . . her daughter has now got a big lump on her face as well and she's only ten," continued Mabel lazily.

"Another big nose?"

"No, just the one big one."

"It seems the big nose runs in the family."

Well with that, Irene was hard pressed to contain her laughter. She sidled up to Milly and whispered in her ear.

"Don't worry Milly, they are quite harmless and are great fun but their dementia makes it difficult for them to think straight."

Milly was thinking that she was in the world of the insane and that Robbie would fit in well with his irritable customer relations. She took out a barley sugar sweet and sucked on it.

Irene took a deep breath and faced the two almost catatonic women.

"OK ladies. Now did you know about the free gift that I will be giving out on Tuesday?" she asked brightly.

"How much is that?" asked Sally.

"She said it was free . . . so it won't cost much at all," replied Mabel sternly.

Irene was getting a bit anxious now as the shop was filling.

"So, I'll see you both Tuesday then?" asked Irene.

With that Sally and Mabel got up slowly and walked out of the door without saying a word or looking at Irene. They were fixated on going to the pub – even though they didn't drink.

"Right Milly, let's be having you then," said a much-relieved Irene as she turned up the music.

"You could do with more help here you know," offered Milly.

"Yes, my Julie here is very good now but I may have to take on another, maybe an apprentice this time."

Once Milly's hair was wet and shampooed, she sat back in her chair and waited for the cutting. Two women, Doris and Enid were making small-talk behind her. Doris had her little girl Sam with her, who was playing up a bit, knocking over the magazine rack and making an irritating screaming noise.

"I'll tan yer hide yer little monster. Now go and get yer haircut from that nice young lady over there like I told you!"

"A went to school wiv her Doris," said Enid quietly.

"Who love?"

"Tanya Hyde. She was a real piece of work that one."

"I wonder if she got called names like, what with a name like that?" asked Doris with a laugh.

"Oh yeah . . . kids were always smackin' her bottom . . . mocking her wiv them names and all that. Tan yer hide . . . yeah, all that. and more."

"Why was that then Enid? Was she a naughty little thing . . . or was she of a particularly dusty appearance?"

"Nah, I think she had circulation problems . . . what wiv them tight clothes and all."

Doris thought for a moment.

"More likely a problem socializing it would seem . . . in tight clothing, so as she couldn't walk straight, I suppose."

"Nah, I think she was straight but she had bad eyes . . . bad teeth . . . bad feet . . . oh and she smoked all day," replied Enid.

"When was that then?"

"Down the road there . . . when I went to St Mary's Primary."

"Blimey. How old was she?"

"Ten going on eleven at the time. Her favourite hobby was stamp collecting. She used to knock people over and stamp all over their lunch, or their heads sometimes."

"Little mongrel eh. So, what's she doin' now then. Have you seen her around?"

"She got herself sorted and changed like, from an ugly duckling into a skanky swan. She got a government job alright she did."

"Doin' what?"

"Foreign Affairs. She was always good at doin' that sort of stuff . . . later on like."

Milly was now wide eyed, thinking that her Eric was growing up with ferals and larger-than-life unhinged characters that were bringing children into the world . . . her world.

She vowed to change hairdressers where normal people went, until she realised that this was normal for the village of Dogbol where she now lived - a place where her parents wouldn't last a day.

Glancing at the bus stop where some local children were hanging around playing a somewhat unusual kicking and spitting game, Milly frantically reached for her phone to call Robbie.

"What's happening Milly, have you got fixed up at the hairdressers?" said a happy sounding, Robbie.

"I've had my hair styled if that's what you mean, yes. Look is there any chance you can pick me up. It's one o'clock now and I have to get that Russian gentleman settled into suite three."

"Oh, he's already here and I've put him into suite eight . . . I couldn't read your scribbly writing. I'm sure it was an eight. Anyhow he's gone out now and so has that Chinese woman, Tian. I don't think they like each other very much," replied Robbie quickly.

"Well, I suppose suite eight has been cleaned anyway. So, can you pick me up then? I need to get back quickly, very quickly."

"I'll be there in ten minutes love. Oh, I'm glad you met the locals love. We couldn't have picked a better place to live."

A grinning Robbie looked at the reservation note and quickly threw it in the bin. He called out to Eric who was in the kitchen looking for a snack in between meals.

"Eric, can you look after things while I pick up your Mum?"

"Sure Dad, I'll sit in reception with my lunch."

"What are you having?"

"Oh, just a sandwich and cold drink," replied Eric hastily.

From the front door Robbie could see Eric scurrying into reception, hiding what looked like a huge double-steak burger and an ice-cold beer.

Robbie estimated that it would have been cheaper to send him to boarding school . . . in Australia.

PR at the DRIP

Security was tight at the Defence Research Industry plant located just outside the village of Dogbol for the special open day planned to showcase the 'AI Soldier' capabilities.

The secret research areas were in lock-down as the media, military personnel, foreign buyers and government agencies were seated strategically for the public display.

A few robot-looking machines were lined up for the guests to view whilst awaiting their debut into the public arena. Of course, they didn't work without having a team of engineers to direct their motion and to make them have a decent conversation by typing in the answers to the public's questions.

Roger Davis was incognito as a dog handler patrolling the back and sides to the event area with Rex. He loved dear old Rex.

He already knew which seats to watch because the facial recognition scans of entrants had picked up on the likes of Ilya Kasparov, Jin Shi Tian and two of the Cigar Club members.

The leader of the Cigar Club, Sir Rodney who was also the director of the DRI plant, kept himself busy socialising with the other elite individuals in attendance.

He was born into the 'elite' with money, title and a society wife, using his position to accumulate more power and wealth.

Although he had some administrative authorisation, he was certainly not a part of any scientific, research or weapons design teams, thereby not requiring intelligence security clearance.

Cartwright, his backup was a very clever I.T. expert who excelled in breaching intranet systems with spectacular Worms and Trojans to extract information or deposit false data.

Today though was just a day when everyone looked at everyone else to see who were the players and who were just posers. The saying that 'you can judge a person by the company they keep' was at the heart of knowing who these people knew – and to add them to your own list of influential friends.

The display was just a distraction for working out who would be willing to spend millions of pounds on as yet unfinished research projects based on some spectacular whimsical ideas.

The interactive presentations all went well of course because the so-called AI Soldiers were backed up by manual remote control should anything need to be 'corrected'.

Cartwright had other things to do, which was secretly scanning for any Internet or Intranet leakages which may be giving away important passwords. The 'Internet of Things' also meant that security cameras, smart phones, vehicle computers and any other lifestyle toys could be the wedge to open the door to the secret vaults of attendees.

It also works the other way. The DRI plant was honing in on Cartwright's scanner, even though he kept moving around – a situation not unnoticed by Roger Davis.

As Davis was moving closer to Cartwright, intending to use the dog to keep him seated, another figure moved in front of him.

"Cartwright, we need your expertise at the podium end. Do you mind? One for all, and orfur . . . none?" said Sir Rodney with a laugh and looking sideways at Davis.

Cartwright got up and went with Sir Rodney, dropping his small intercepting device onto the floor between the feet of a female government agent. He had destroyed the device with his ring.

Davis and the dog were gaining ground just as two security team members approached the woman.

"Excuse me but can you please come with us and don't panic, please, it is just a routine security drill," one of them asked the woman politely. She quickly showed him her high-level agency clearance tag.

Davis showed the security his own credentials. The security team nodded and left with puzzled smiles.

"So, Elizabeth, you have been chosen as a depositary for some second-hand scanning gear. Do you mind handing it to me please before we all create a scene for the media?"

"I might have known it was something to do with you Roger. Anyway, there's nothing anyone can get away with today . . . everything is switched off," she replied with a smile.

"Even switched off equipment can be hacked Liz. Such is the race to see who is the cleverest in the field. Anyway at least I know that the man is a player . . . and who his friends are. That's a step ahead of the pack for now."

"Can I help you with anything else?" she asked seductively.

"Just keep your eyes out for positions B6 and T14. The Russians and Chinese are here to gain whatever information they can and I'm sure some of the business people here today have their own interests at stake as well. It is information that we want at the moment too. See who they talk to."

Davis went for another walk around the perimeter with the dog. A tall man approached him.

"Hello Mr Davis, it is nice day for walking doggie," said Kasparov.

Davis was not surprised at this face-to-face encounter.

"Well Ilya, I forget what rank you are these days . . . probably General by now. I find it therapeutic to have a friend that I can trust to follow orders . . . and all he wants is a bone. Don't let your diplomatic pass misguide you into thinking that you are immune from being detained."

Kasparov laughed aloud before looking down at where the dog had urinated on his trousers and shoes.

"Yep, I think my friend Rex here agrees," continued Davis.

Davis moved off to see what Jin Shi Tian was up to.

"May I see your pass please? Just a routine security check Madame," asked Davis with a wry smile.

Tian looked a little miffed that she had been singled out just to ruffle her feathers a little amongst other attendees. Blowing her cover would mean that certain 'elements' in the crowd would now avoid her.

"What a nice dog," she said, touching the dog's head lightly and showing Davis her Diplomatic Status pass.

Rex looked unusually calm and even friendly.

"Ah, another Diplomatic Pass. But I must point out that any meddling with internal trade or military research information between our two countries may see you overstaying your welcome . . . at her majesties request. I can't search you but I do know that you probably have some photographs of the people attending here today."

Tian got up ready to leave after her pass was returned and made a brief comment before disappearing quickly into the distance.

"It's not what you see that is important, but what you can't see even as it happens. This is because you sleep on the job Mr Davis."

About five minutes later Davis noticed that the dog was very quiet. In fact, Rex was soundly asleep.

"This will be hard to explain," mumbled Davis to himself, rubbing his chin.

Elizabeth walked past and laughed at his predicament.

"It's better than having an embarrassed dog watching over a sleeping agent."

Eric Steps Up

With the DRIP show over, both Tian and Ilya returned to the Mayfair Mews hotel, crossing paths in the foyer.

"Ah Madame, did I not see you at the show today?"

Tian looked at him and then at his discoloured trouser bottoms. She sniffed the air briefly before giving him a sympathetic smile.

"It seems we met the same Mr Davis and his delightful dog today Mr . . . Kasparov, yes? Maybe we can have dinner together and I can tell you a little about my business here."

"Yes Madame Jin, I wish we had such dogs in Russia to control the crowds . . . and please call me Ilya. Oh, and yes, I would love to have you for dinner," said Kasparov slowly, choosing his words carefully.

"And I am called Tian, please. What about seven o'clock then as it now only five?"

"Seven is good . . . and now I must unpack and get settled," replied Kasparov.

They both moved on just as Eric was entering the foyer from the kitchen, wiping crumbs from his mouth.

Milly was at reception and Robbie was picking up another guest from Doulton.

"I'm just going to go around to Ruby's house to see if I can persuade her to have a meal here Mum," shouted Eric on his way out.

Mum liked Ruby and encouraged Eric to 'bring her out of her shell' a bit. They both went to the same school and probably the same college this next year.

Ruby however was quite anxious in company, giving the impression that she hated everyone. She did actually hate nearly everyone, which cemented the cycle of reciprocal un-liking.

She was very smart and was often teased because of her hidden good looks and witty abusive comments.

At school she joined some of the nerdy activities with such unlikely titles as 'forensic thinking', 'strategies of war' and 'hacking computer networks'. She also went to some physical exercise classes – but no one else knew what she did there.

Of course, these activities were based on her knowing how and what methods are used by criminals, in order to prevent being a victim of such scams and tricks herself. But if you know some of it, a smart person will learn a lot more. Ruby knew heaps!

Eric was more of a creative inventor of solutions which was the main reason that Ruby thought she hated him.

He would solve the same problems by intuitive logic rather than by Ruby's systematic analysis using previous similar solutions.

Their worlds were about to collide in an avalanche of intrigue.

Roger Davis, as all intelligence officers will tell you was trained in the art of collecting information. Now you can digitally collect information from people and things and he had the things; surveillance gadgets and the like . . . but he didn't have the people in place at the Mayfair Mews hotel.

Any of his own people would be easily recognised or noticed by their looks and how they acted. What was needed was an insider . . . or two.

Eric ran down the road to Ruby's house but was bailed up by a man standing beside a white van.

"Hi there, can I have a word with you for just a brief moment?" asked the stranger.

"Sure, what can I help you with?"

The stranger showed him a government agency security tag and introduced himself as Roger Davis.

And so started a pleasant conversation initially about school, college, university before proceeding to paint what may lay ahead for a person with a mind such as his.

"But you don't know much about me at all. I haven't really done anything yet," said Eric.

"Ah, but that's where you are mistaken Eric. I know everything about you, your parents, your hotel and even about some of your guests. So, what I'm asking is that you help me to do my job at protecting our country by just casually monitoring two of your guests. Just simple things like when they come and go, who they see, what you may hear or see.

Quite safe and above board and it would certainly help your case for working in a government position when you graduate. Oh, and I must stress that you can't tell your parents, or friends for that matter."

Eric thought about the possibilities and the excitement of being a real-life spy, working for his country. Then his imagination kicked into a fanciful daydream where he visualised that he would one day save Ruby from some foreign intrigue and win her over. That was the deciding factor alright!

"Count me in Mr Davis . . . er do I get a code name or something to protect my identity when giving information?"

Davis was ecstatic at having his surveillance covered and promptly came up with a name that was sure to be much admired and respected by Eric and maybe his future operatives.

"You will be known as 'Diamond' and I will be your only contact."

"Diamond . . . Wow! That sounds very suitable for when I go out with . . . er, for when I go out on surveillance. A hard stone so polished and refined . . . with a high value and multi-faceted perspective. Hang on then. So do I get paid for doing that?" asked Eric as he re-focussed on the real-world values.

Davis was taken aback and then thought more about the high value that his information would unearth.

"Yes Eric, you will be paid, according to the information received and its worth to us. Now make sure you act normally and have dinner in the restaurant at seven tonight. You will be our eyes and ears on the Russian Kasparov and that Chinese lady, Madame Jin or Tian as she prefers. I will contact you . . . 'Diamond' in the near future."

Eric was on cloud nine as Davis sped off in his van, singing loudly to himself, tapping the beat on the steering wheel.

As he approached Ruby's house, Eric felt like he was empowered to knock the door down, carry her off in his arms and take her to dinner by force. But then he remembered that she also took karate classes and would probably have no qualms about killing him outright or maiming him in a most distasteful fashion.

Ruby was coming out of her house and could see Eric going through the motions of his daydreaming.

"Are you alright Eric? You seem to be having trouble walking."

Eric breathed in and became Diamond again.

"Ruby . . . Ruby, I want to ask you if you will have dinner with me tonight at the restaurant . . . and . . . and I will not take no for an answer," blurted out Eric.

Without hesitation and with the most casual, laid-back poise, Ruby replied softly.

"Why yes, that would be very nice Eric. What, say about seven o'clock so that I can get changed into something more . . . suitable?"

Apart from being knocked out by getting a positive reply, Eric calculated that Ruby had a whopping two hours to get ready.

What would take that long? He looked at her long hair, loose top and baggy jeans. He re-focussed on her face.

"Why yes, great . . . great . . . well I'll be seeing you there then."

"But surely you are going to call around to pick me up?" she replied in a now high-tension and louder voice.

"Yes of course, that was the idea. I was just thinking of when we actually get there . . . together . . . at the same time. Bye for now . . . err."

"Ruby! . . . Ruby," she sighed.

Ruby relaxed a little, well a lot actually thinking about the money she had just saved, given to her by her parents to buy her dinner at the restaurant because they would be home late.

They really wanted her to treat herself in the hope of meeting up with Eric. Coaxing Ruby to like Eric was like walking on thin ice.

Eric's Mum and Ruby's parents thought that Eric and Ruby was a match made in heaven. The big trick was not to actually tell them that. The deception was that none of them knew if that was in fact remotely true.

Eric's Dad also wanted Eric to like Ruby or any girl for that matter . . . then to immediately marry the girl and move far away from his hotel business.

"You'd like Australia lad," he would often say, showing him brochures on emigration.

I Spy

There was a lot of thoughts spinning through Eric's mind as he sat on the porch steps, dressed in his best casuals, looking out at a world full of opportunity and surprises.

Why, in one day he had secured a date with the elusive and often reclusive Ruby and was now called 'Diamond' by the British Secret Service – and he was still only sixteen, well nearly seventeen.

Out of all the excitement he could only focus on Ruby, realising he had a fascination with her that he could not explain in simple words.

She was tall, slim with long hair and beneath her heavy glasses and long fringe he knew that she was hiding his perfect girlfriend. But apart from all that, her presence made him feel weak at the knees and he longed for her to be closer to him. Maybe it was the lingering orange blossom perfume that drifted around her and clung to all her possessions.

He snapped out of his daydream.

"The car . . . the car! I don't even have a licence and I have to pick her up in thirty minutes," cried Eric, waking up from his consuming thoughts.

Luck was on his side yet again.

Robbie was coming out to see him, to find out exactly how Ruby was going to get to the hotel with his son sitting idly outside staring into the distance.

"Dad, I forgot to make arrangements to get Ruby to the hotel and I don't want to just walk up with her. She deserves better than that."

Robbie put his hand on Eric's shoulder and smiled.

"Why can't you just tell her how you feel about her and see what happens lad? At least you'll know, for better or for worse. But what I've come to tell you is that I can not only drive you and Ruby to the hotel, but tonight I have Joe Finch's Mercedes Benz for a wedding tomorrow . . . so you can have a grand ride and a grand night."

Eric jumped up and thanked his Dad as they both headed towards the beautiful black Mercedes Saloon parked around the corner.

Eric's mind was in overdrive as he stared at the perfect ride.

"Hurry up, get in and let's show Ruby what a stylish young man has come to be taking out such a special girl for an evening out."

Eric settled into the leather seat at the front and closed his eyes. Today was a special day indeed. Maybe even the turning point in his sheltered life.

The Mercedes roared into life, mainly because Robbie liked the feel of revving the engine and just sitting there in Park position, imagining what Milly would say if he had bought such a car.

How he would love this car for himself . . . and of course the hotel would then be able to cater for formal weddings, picking up guests in a most suitable luxury motor vehicle.

"Dad, are we going now? It's almost time to pick up Ruby."

"Oh, sorry Eric, I was just fantasising about owning a car like this," replied Robbie.

"There's one for sale at Lambert's Car Yard in Doulton. Why don't you take a look and see what they'll give you for the Lexus?"

Dad's mind was racing but he didn't say any more until they reached Ruby's house. She was waiting at the gate. At least they thought it must be her . . . and then she turned around!

A tall, willowy young woman in a stunning red dress . . . and red lipstick!

"Whoa! Man alive, who or what is that stunning girl over there?" shouted Eric to his father, partly ecstatic and partly out of fear that it may not even be Ruby . . . but then it was her house.

"Looks like a million dollars to me Eric. Who would have known eh . . . and she has spent some time preparing to be your date tonight too. Quick, go over to her and then open the car door for her. Quickly now before she walks over."

Ruby was smiling and held out her hand for Eric to lead her to the car. However, Eric being the son of Robbie reached out and shook her hand, causing Ruby to laugh.

"Wow Ruby, I can hardly recognise you. Your fringe and glasses are gone and your hair is just so . . . perfect!"

Ruby mouthed something which Eric sensed in slow motion as she grabbed his hand and pulled him over to where the car was parked. Eric was in a trance.

"Hello Mr Johnson, thank you for picking me up. This is such a beautiful car."

"Hello Ruby. My goodness, I am surprised at just how much you have grown up and blossomed into an extremely beautiful young woman. The Mercedes was Eric's idea, as he thought you deserved the best. Oh, and the chef is preparing a nice menu special for you after Eric found out what you like."

Eric helped Ruby into the plush back seat of the car and ran around to the other side to get in, bewildered as to what his father was saying. Then he ran around to her side again to close the door, much to the amusement of both Ruby and Robbie.

"Thank you for the flowers, Eric, they are so beautiful and a nice thought," said Ruby clutching a small spray of multi-coloured flowers with a central red rose.

"Oh, yes . . . I thought you would like them Ruby and they certainly match your dress . . . and eyes and everything!"

Robbie looked at Eric in the rear-view mirror with a smile.

"You look great too Eric. I like your shirt and those suede shoes are superb. You look so smart and cool."

Eric felt very excited and yet humbled at the same time as he realised that Ruby just might like him after all, and that his own reserved attention to her was the reason she had appeared uninterested.

The Mayfair Mews hotel looked a pretty site at night with an arrangement of street lighting and decorative fixtures, painting a scene straight out of the movies.

Eric jumped out of the car and opened the door for Ruby. When she stood next to him, he could feel her warmth. Then the orange blossom wafted all around him like a narcotic velvet scarf.

Robbie drove the car around the back and headed into the kitchen to see if chef had arranged everything.

Milly had been at reception and on seeing the Mercedes pull up was waiting at the front door to usher Ruby and Eric into the restaurant.

"Hello Ruby. My, what a beautiful dress and just look how gorgeous you are tonight too. Why I remember you when we first came here and were only six years old," gushed Milly.

"Thank you Mrs Johnson. I am so thrilled to be dining with Eric in your restaurant. You are all like a second family to me."

Two more diners were arriving at the restaurant and their accents caused Eric to freeze and forget Ruby for a moment.

Ruby noticed his reaction with interest.

Milly went to greet the other diners.

"Mr Kasparov and Tian, I hope you are settled in well and that you will find something of interest on our menu tonight. Chef has been preparing some special dishes and our wine list has been enhanced with some new wines that we tasted whilst in France only last year."

"Thank you Milly for your kind words and yes we will enjoy your food and wine tonight I'm sure," replied Kasparov gently.

"Yes, thank you Milly. We met at an exhibition today and thought we could compare notes over a nice dinner," added Tian.

Milly led them to a table next to Eric and Ruby where they all offered a quick greeting. Ruby looked very impressed with the way Tian had dressed . . . like from a James Bond movie she thought.

Eric looked petrified, so much so that Ruby decided to settle him down a bit.

"I feel a little nervous tonight, Eric, so please don't think that I'm not enjoying our evening together," offered Ruby.

Eric looked at her and melted. He knew she was offering some help for whatever was bothering him.

"I'm sorry for being a bit edgy. I should have told you especially, that there is something else that is on my mind . . . that you should possibly know about."

"Can you tell me now? I mean is it anything to do with you and me going out?"

"Absolutely not! Honestly Ruby, it is something that I can't tell you here, now, but I will after dinner, I assure you. In fact, I will not even think about what it is or start my . . . operation . . . until we have talked," he ushered ever quieter.

"Operation . . . are you ill . . . or dying? . . . Oh my god you're dying!" said Ruby with a louder voice.

Both Tian and Kasparov looked around briefly on hearing that word. It was something that came up quite regularly in their work.

"Goodness me. No! Please let's just quieten down a little and enjoy our meal and then I will tell you. You will be surprised alright . . . and it will be of interest to you, what with your school activities and all," hinted Eric with more confidence and a reassuring smile.

Ruby decided it was probably some silly 'boy thing' and that she would find the whole surprise quite boring in the end.

Anyway, she was feeling hungry after all the fussing and after a preliminary drink they ordered from the magnificently adorned menu.

Eric decided not to bother with his spying duties for a while, as there was a more pressing engagement to occupy his mind and soul. In fact, he realised that he was actually living his daydream.

From that moment on, the Russians and Chinese could mount an all-out world war but he would be away with his thoughts . . . and with his new girlfriend, Ruby Peters.

As it turned out, both Kasparov and Tian received urgent messages on their phones almost within a minute of each other. They both quickly examined their messages and looked at each other's nervousness in remaining at the restaurant.

"I'm afraid that I must go to an urgent meeting with my superiors Ilya and I hope that you may excuse me . . . and that we can arrange another time for our get together," prompted Tian touching his hand lightly.

"Da, I also have the same predicament and was afraid that if I stay any longer, they may send someone to shoot me," laughed Kasparov quietly.

They both had a laugh, got up and went to Milly to apologise for their departure.

Eric reached into his pocket, took out a notebook and scribbled a quick note, trying to hide his clumsy antics from Ruby who was looking at him curiously.

"It's seven ten if you want to write that down as well," offered Ruby, looking quite annoyed.

"Just a little note for tomorrow, Ruby. I'll tell you later."

Robbie was entering the reception area as the two guests were leaving and had a quiet word with Milly.

"What's with our foreign guests love?"

"Oh, they both had to leave for meetings. At least they are here for four weeks and will have plenty of time to eat at the restaurant."

Robbie peered over the half-swing doors into the restaurant.

"Looks like Eric and Ruby are hitting it off."

"Yes, it's only taken ten years for them to get closer," replied Milly.

"Who would have thought she would look like that . . . what with the dress, makeup and the fancy hairdo eh love."

Milly smiled at him and shook her head.

"She is also a very smart young lady too. She could probably teach us all a thing or two about surviving modern life."

Robbie nodded his head in agreement which surprised Milly.

"She needs to be a survivor alright if Eric doesn't start pulling his weight by taking on more responsibilities," said Robbie.

They both looked at Eric and Ruby enjoying their meal and leaning closer to each other, obviously whispering private words of close affection.

Now that the two spies had left the restaurant, Eric took hold of Ruby's hands and looked deeply into her eyes.

Ruby was unsure about this sudden attention and yet waited for what he had to say. She was geared up to attack at the slightest provocation – an instinct instilled into her by her karate teacher.

"Listen very closely Ruby and please . . . don't laugh because what I'm going to tell you is true. In fact, I'm not supposed to tell anyone."

Ruby was intrigued because she also had something to tell Eric and Ruby's senses were telling her that Eric was more than he seemed.

"Those two people who were in here just now are foreign spies," he started.

Ruby's eyes narrowed.

"Really!"

"And I have been chosen . . . to be an intelligence officer . . . for the British Government . . . to see what they are up to . . . and they have given me a codename of . . . Diamond!" he continued dramatically, full of importance.

Eric waited for a response which was not short in coming.

Ruby's eyes narrowed even further and a grimace, no maybe a scowl had appeared on her apparently angry face.

He felt a sharp kick under the table, right into his shin, but before he had a chance to say anything, Ruby nodded her head slowly as if acknowledging a whopper of a story had just been told.

Yet that was not what she was thinking!

"Well Diamond boy . . . you have just blown your cover, unmasked two spies and put both our lives . . . more importantly mine, in great danger! Why, I could have dispensed with your life in two seconds!"

"What? What are you talking about . . . Ruby?" he stammered.

Ruby sat back in her chair and folded her arms, then leaned across the table and flicked water from the rinsing bowl into his face.

"I have also been approached by that slimy, slippery Davis character into doing exactly the same thing . . . and I didn't get a codename either," she continued raising her voice.

Eric was deflated and embarrassed.

"Well, you are called Ruby . . . that's a good enough name," he gestured lightly.

Ruby sat back in her chair again and thought about the position she was now in.

She wanted Eric to be her boyfriend after many years of getting him to show some interest and now they were embarking on a dangerous journey into the unknown . . . apparently together . . . dealing with agents unknown with possibly false papers, IDs and agendas that could affect their entire families.

"Look Eric . . . first off, I thought you wanted to take me out because you liked me. Now I find out that you are interfering in my operation that was private and involved no-one except me."

Eric took hold of her hands.

"Quite frankly Ruby, the fear of telling you that I love you has passed, what with all these goings on . . ."

"You do . . . you love me?" whispered Ruby.

"Yes, I do, and I have for a long time, but you've always been so distant with me . . . and yet I can't get you out of my mind."

Ruby's smile and glistening eyes made Eric think quickly about his days as Diamond. Well, he was sort of a spy for a day anyway. He would give it up now in return for the love of Ruby.

But wait! He now knew that Ruby was up for it as well, so what was she going to do about that he wondered.

"Wait on Ruby. Let's look at this calmly and logically. I think you still like me, but I need to know it . . . and this spying business needs to be sorted out. The fact that we both fell for the 'Agent of England' caper means that we obviously believed in doing it."

Ruby dabbed her eyes with the napkin and thought about what Eric had said and what she wanted to do about it.

"Yes, I like you a lot Eric . . . I'm not sure if it is love at this stage, but I'm always thinking about you . . . you are very distracting and I like being with you. Then this matter of spying comes up. Well, if you can call it that. I mean it is only giving basic information to our own government agency after all. In fact because Davis knows that we have both been approached by him, then a problem shared is a problem halved. We can work together as a team and at the same time be less conspicuous!"

Eric had come to the same conclusion although he was beginning to think that Ruby was starting to act like his boss.

"That's a grand idea Ruby . . . for starters. We cover each other's backs," replied Eric sounding like a movie star.

"Well, I know karate . . . what do you do?" said Ruby jokingly.

"Well, I can clean up the joint once you've finished," replied Eric with a wide grin.

They both laughed.

"Now what are you having for dessert Ruby."

"Hmmm, I may go for the pavlova . . . as long as you taste it first and keep your knife on the table where I can see it."

Their new line of banter lasted all evening amid some occasional staring into each other's eyes.

When they were done, Eric signalled to his father that they were nearly ready to go home. Ruby fumbled about in her purse.

"Here Eric, it is the modern age and I would like to pay for half of the dinner."

Eric looked at her and shook his head. Then he became serious.

"Ok then, well let's see now, entree, main course, sweets, drinks . . . oh, that will probably come to about . . ."

Ruby's eyes widened. She also had her mouth wide open.

"And then half of that . . . and with VAT as well and my personal charge for being your bodyguard, that would be near enough to zero too. I mean the meal is on the restaurant Ruby, so we can thank my parents for that."

Ruby sidled up beside him and gave him the softest of kisses on the cheek, leaving a bright red lipstick mark. This was not missed by Robbie and Milly who nearly fell through the door they were hiding behind.

"I should have bought two one-way tickets to Australia love," joked Robbie.

Milly punched him in the ribs but couldn't stop smiling.

"I'll send for the car Ruby," stammered Eric catching his leg on the table and his hand on the flower vase. Ruby caught it before it reached the ground – which completely amazed Eric.

Robbie was already heading out to fetch the car as Milly greeted them at the restaurant door.

"So, did you enjoy your meal, you two?"

"Mrs Johnson that was the most incredible meal of my entire life . . . and I especially enjoyed Eric's company."

"Thanks Mum. That was a very nice gesture letting us both have an expensive three course meal with all the trimmings."

"Call me Milly from now on Ruby . . . and Eric you'll be able to pay us back out of your wages this summer . . . only kidding love," replied Milly with a tear in her eye.

Eric had never been so happy. Ruby was smiling because she not only had a new boyfriend but had saved a substantial amount of money that would now buy her some more clothes.

Robbie came back to usher them into the car.

"Thank you Mr Johnson for a wonderful night at the hotel."

"Robbie will do from now on Ruby and I'm glad that you had a good time. I'm pleased that Eric behaved himself and didn't turn out to be a . . . rough diamond . . . on your first date . . . eh lad," said Robbie with an air of mystery.

Both Ruby and Eric thought briefly about his choice of words and the way he said them. Looking sideways at each other they both mouthed 'no way'.

The trip back to Ruby's house was much too short as they were accompanied by Robbie who would look at them briefly in the rear-vision mirror.

Eric whisked around to Ruby's door and pulled her out of the car to her front door, just out of view of Robbie.

Eric took another long look into Ruby's eyes and planted a tender kiss on her sweet soft lips, then held her close.

Ruby opened her mouth and pushed him gently away.

"Yes, I do . . . think I love you Eric and I think that we can be good for each other. Thank you for such a great evening and I will dream about this all night. Now I think your father's waiting to take you home."

Eric smiled at her as his cheeky side came through.

"You know your karate lessons are a real incentive to keep things nice and slow," he said flippantly.

Ruby made a quick flick of her hands and leg as if to incapacitate him making Eric duck and jump backwards, nearly falling over.

"Just remember that, Diamond!"

They both laughed and Eric looked back, nearly tripping over a stone as he slowly made his way to the waiting car.

"Love all," whispered Robbie to his love-struck son, with the trip back in total silence.

Eric thought about his most wonderful day, in the quiet space that his father knew he needed.

"They would love Australia at this time of year," whispered Robbie to himself.

Data Hack

It was an interesting night for Kasparov, Tian and Davis as word had got around that there had been an Intranet hack at the Ministry of Defence (M.O.D.) with particular reference to the Defence Research Institute plant in Dogbol.

Initially each agency watchdog monitors the 'buzz' and then informs their superiors for transmission to field agents.

The spoken words Dog, Bowl, Drip and Meeb coming from an as yet unknown source had even the most serious of agents having to reach for their acronym guide books. The signal appeared to be coming from Saudi Arabia and the speaker had a particularly strong accent.

As most Western Intelligence gets re-directed to Australia, they were the first outside of Britain to attempt to decipher it.

Half past seven was a busy period for informing agents about the new development.

"Dog Bowl, what the hell is that?" asked Joe Goldberg from the American CIA centre in Pine Gap, Australia.

"Reckon the 'dog' part is pretty obvious. Ah, ya know mate, like 'a dingo's got my baby' scenario, and maybe 'bowl' is a code word for a consortium, intent on kidnapping someone at a facility in Pommy Land." offered David Reichmann, ASIO counterpart, with no part, but a lot of counter to rest his feet on.

"Well, if you're sure then, inform Washington that the Brits will be on alert for a kidnapping, and get our London agents out there asking around to see who could be involved. It could be us next time and we want to know who these people are."

"Shall I let the Brits know through Joint Intelligence, Joe?" asked David hesitantly.

David shrugged his shoulders and looked peeved.

"Send GCHQ a cryptic message like: Intercepted vocal 'comms' on your patch. Key words are Dog, Bowl, Dripping and Dingo, relating to possible kidnapping."

They both laughed and shook their heads.

Meanwhile the Russians and Chinese had immediately linked the words Dogbol and DRIP to the current offering of secret papers from the Cigar Club in London and had summoned their field agents Kasparov and Jin Shi Tian respectively to embassy meetings. By eight o'clock that night, their urgent calls made to Sir Rodney, confirmed the fact that the Cigar Club had indeed hacked some crucial information from DRIP. He had been waiting patiently to see how long it would take for his 'players' to contact him.

"Yes, we have some site layouts, passwords, project names and personnel details," Sir Rodney oozed to tempt each caller.

Then he would keep quiet as they would savagely start throwing money and possibly a few threats around in order to secure the information solely for themselves.

The Cigar Club was summoned for another meeting at nine o'clock sharp, in the morning. Cartwright was told to make sure the information was valid and current. Cartwright was going out on the town to celebrate his girlfriend's birthday.

Now you may be wondering what the British Intelligence was doing at this time – certainly not twiddling their thumbs you would hope. Not wanting to gain the attention of fiction crime writers at least.

Well, Roger Davis was doing exactly that whilst staring at his computer screen, watching the flow of voice data from one London site to some foreign sites which were masked by encryption, diversions via bots and short code.

He had succeeded in dumping some 'almost real' diagrams and folders into an Intranet hard-drive that had purposefully been hacked through the domestic intelligence National Crime Authority (NCA) portal by 'persons unknown' in the Middle East.

The fact that the persons were unknown could be true or false depending on your investment viewpoint. Unknown because they had a fake name; known because it was the NCA themselves; unknown because they didn't tell anyone else; but then known by British Intelligence, especially GCHQ, because that was the whole point of the baiting exercise.

In effect, Davis had dumped a wad of dud plans and documents, reasonably easy to steal, in which to draw out the 'players' and to accumulate evidence against them for future prosecution – or elimination. It is after all a cut-throat business.

So far there were two factions that had "stolen" the information. One of them he knew was the 'Cigar Club'. The other was persons unknown, operating out of the Middle East – probably the Arab University students on behalf of arms traders . . . or maybe Scarab!

Davis also received word from GCHQ about the CIA receiving a deciphered voice message from the Middle East via Pine Gap.

He read the message and structured a suitable return-reply which he read out to himself in between smothered giggles.

"Re warning: PAL worked. Key words Eat, Shorts, Mine."

Bright Gems

It was now eight o'clock in the morning and a ruffled, bleary-eyed Eric was waking from a disturbed sleep. He was late for the school bus that had slowly trawled by outside the hotel expecting the normally impatient schoolboy.

At the back of his mind, two concurrent thoughts were intertwined and fleetingly clear . . . Ruby liked him enough to be kissed, and he was now a poor man's Bond in the guise of 'Diamond' in which his new girlfriend could disable him with one swift kick.

He screwed his nose up and looked at the wall clock.

And that's when he was thrown into the day's normality.

He quickly threw some water on his face, had a quick sniff under his armpit to be satisfied that last night's shower was sufficient; then put on his school uniform.

At least there was only this week of school exams left before the summer holidays – and then college.

"Eric! Come and have some breakfast. The bus has gone and your dad is not around to take you to school," shouted Milly.

Eric dived down the steps from his bedroom located on the first floor of the main building, nearly running into Milly who was carrying a breakfast tray to one of the guests.

"Brush your hair, tuck your shirt in and grab something from the breakfast bar," she rushed, "Oh, and the telecom man has just finished his work on our node in the street . . . and said he'll give you a lift to school."

Eric ran into the restaurant and grabbed some toast and an orange juice from the breakfast bar. On turning around, a heavily clothed figure wearing a bright orange safety vest and a pulled-down tartan cap was standing right behind him casually pointing some half-eaten toast at him.

"You're gonna have to be more punctual than that me old diamond if you're gonna catch them early worms you know," said Davis, pulling the cap further over his eyes.

Eric's heart skipped a beat he was sure, as all the events from the previous day flooded back. He dropped his toast the wrong-way up and was left wide-eyed, open-mouthed and hungry.

Davis chuckled to himself, touched his mouth with a fingerless glove indicating that Eric should remain quiet, and then pointed to the white van outside.

The door of the van opened as they approached and an already shocked Eric was thrown into overdrive by the sight of someone sitting there with folded arms and a mischievous grin.

"Get in Diamond or I'll have to break your legs . . . or kiss you . . . I haven't decided yet," shouted Ruby in a tough gangster voice.

Davis broke into a wide grin.

"Neither option is part of your surveillance duties Ruby even though Eric would I'm sure prefer the latter punishment."

"Ruby, what are you doing here? . . . It's too dangerous to be seen with Mister Davis. Oh my god, what have we let ourselves in for," said a troubled Eric.

Before Ruby could reply, Davis set the record straight.

"Right, both of you! Stop right there and listen to me closely."

Ruby smiled at Eric and made room for him to sit next to her.

"This is not a game and I am sticking my neck out because you are not yet eighteen . . . and technically, asking you to collect any information on your visitors is most likely illegal."

Eric and Ruby looked at each other in a different light.

"All I am asking is that you note the time of day these people come and go . . . but only if you happen to notice . . . note no deliberate spying on them . . . and maybe if you can tell me who picked them up . . . or a car registration. Absolutely no more than that! Do I make myself clear?" continued Davis in a stern voice.

Eric and Ruby nodded.

"Now I'll ask you if you want to continue . . . or else I'll find another way of gaining that information. Are you still in?"

"Yes, I'm still in . . . but I just want to say that I'm sorry for calling you this morning . . . demanding a codename and all that . . . I was very immature and I apologise," said Ruby quietly.

Eric looked at Ruby closely, trying to figure out what codename she would have requested.

"Well, I'm still in as well and promise to be a bit more mature and careful about what I say to people . . . and how I act. Some of my antics were a little bit over the top," said Eric.

Davis looked carefully at each one, sipping the last of his coffee.

Eric leaned back a little and looked at Ruby again sideways. Ruby caught him out and stared back at him, before her frustration reached boiling point.

"Scarlett! OK! Now get over it!" she blurted.

Eric's initial reaction was to look straight ahead but fortune was not smiling on him today as he couldn't contain the widening smirk on his face and his now famous muffled giggle, suppressed by holding his breath.

Ruby somehow managed to kick him in the same shin as the night before.

Davis ignored the goings on with a deep sigh and proceeded to take them both to school. But not before swivelling his side-mirror camera onto a blue Audi parked about one hundred metres away containing at least two persons wearing dark sunglasses – on an overcast day.

As he drove past the car, their car window wound shut but he was still able to get a series of photos anyway. Later analysis would suggest that these people were of Middle Eastern appearance – information that would complicate the entire surveillance operation.

After dropping off his new 'recruits' at the school, Davis was bothered by the thought that these new 'players' had seen him with Eric and Ruby.

He realised that he had made a serious mistake in recruiting them for what was now becoming such a complicated assignment.

He started thinking about an exit plan to keep them both safe and 'off the books' in order to pursue their strangely reminiscent romance. How time flies in a rapid paced world he thought.

A quick glance in his rear-view mirror proved that the other car was still on his tail. Davis pushed his earpiece to communicate with his team.

"Davis on High and Grantham in Doulton with a rather annoying rear tail. Intercept to remove tail but do not approach," ordered Davis casually.

Within one minute two cars were behind Davis making sufficient manoeuvres to prevent the tail from keeping up with him. A quick check on the registration proved to be at least confirmation that the people were from the Saudi embassy . . . or at least the car was registered to them. The embassy car sped off at the next turn.

Back at the hotel, Kasparov was finishing off his breakfast in his room whilst talking in coded Russian to his embassy using an encrypted mobile phone.

"The first chapter of Sir Rodney's book is for sale and I have concluded that we should buy this for say a round million, even though my counterpart is probably drinking her green tea and organising the same thing for a higher price."

The reply was short.

"You transfer and I collect . . . usual time, place . . . and send Natasha to swap at airport cafe", continued Kasparov.

Again, the reply must have been only one sentence.

"Cigars . . . cigars! I must have some more for baiting and resuming contact," replied Kasparov angrily.

He looked out of the front window of his suite to see Madame Jin walking towards a dark blue Bentley. The door was opened by a formal chauffeur. He could see a Chinese gentleman sitting in the back apparently smiling at him.

"Hello Chinese man . . . I have a nice photograph of your smiling face for my collection," murmured Kasparov.

Then he thought about calling a mere taxi to pick him up.

It was at that moment he realised that the scale of money offerings between the two rival countries was very apparent by the way their field agents got around.

"I would be asking two million from Chinese," he thought.

He called reception to find Milly answering in her usual polite, friendly style and was slightly compensated by the fact that Robbie was on his way back to the hotel and would immediately take him to the airport.

Meanwhile at the school, Eric was sitting his physics exam, concentrating on the task at hand and putting all his day dreaming on hold. Once he was locked into a desire to show the school his prowess in passing all his subjects, Eric could not be distracted.

Similarly, Ruby was a smart and adept student when it came to exams, but unlike Eric she could still hold on to thoughts and memories that mattered to her. One such thought was the realisation that Eric was in love with her and she remembered well the soft kiss on the lips. That was the theorem proof she needed.

She now had an air of confidence and maturity that was starting to ruffle her school friends – always jealous of her schoolwork and hidden charm. She was showing this apparent air of superiority that girls don't seem to like about each other, unless they are the ones who have been conniving enough to be thought of as the group leader.

Boys on the contrary just rough it out and hope to be more casual, laid-back and well just 'normally low profile'.

Ruby's mathematics exam was a breeze as expected. Having mastered the theory and practical application of components far above her school level, she loved the induction, deduction and analysis of mathematical unknowns – much like the way she had analysed Eric and discovered his hidden passion for excitement and . . . now romance.

She smiled again at her worst enemy, Rosemary Winters who she called 'blizzard face', who promptly ran to her group members for consolation. Just to bring things to a head, Eric was walking up to the bus stop where the group was standing.

Ruby went straight up to him and gave him a long kiss on the lips which made Eric weak at the knees to the point of collapsing.

Luckily, Ruby was holding onto him tight to keep him upright.

The look on those girl's faces will remain with Ruby forever as a life-changing moment of her growing up and standing tall against adversity.

Eric however will remember it as the day his friends shouted and jeered at him as if he had been forced by a girl group bet to make him overcome his previous shyness and awkwardness around girls.

Eric did recover and learnt very quickly how to tolerate such an outpouring of emotion from his Ruby, to the extent that he welcomed such an event to explode at any time.

As the school bus was about to set off for Dogbol, Robbie's taxi was going the opposite way heading for the airport.

Robbie and Kasparov were getting on quite well considering neither liked small-talk. Robbie was asking about Russian life in general and commented that Kasparov spoke English extremely well.

It is amazing how a taxi driver can make passengers feel at ease – or extremely hostile – all depending on their manner and charm.

A guarded Kasparov was happy to talk about his homeland and indicated that he missed the scenery and especially the food.

"You are good taxi driver Robbie," he continued, "most only speak of weather and cricket score. Maybe we can rob bank together and you can drive us in getaway car."

Robbie looked across at him with a grin.

"The weather is generally crap here and we seem to be losing the cricket . . . so why wouldn't I want to know more about my passengers . . . just in case I want to emigrate. No place can be worse than winter in Dog Bowl."

Kasparov thought it was a fair comment.

"So why do you not change name from Dog Bowl to something more exotic at least. I hear your wife say Dodge Bull . . . but to me this is still funny name, yes? Why do your English names always have to be funny . . . like Mouse Hole and Wooster Share?"

Robbie laughed with Kasparov as they were turning into the airport drop-off point.

"Surely you're not leaving for home already Ilya just to eat some home-cooked food?"

"No, no Robbie, just meeting an old, old friend who will be returning home today," he replied casually.

A strikingly beautiful blonde woman in a fur coat and fur hat was waiting at the entrance taking Robbie by surprise.

"Maybe that is my next fare . . . I hope," said Robbie as Kasparov left the taxi.

Kasparov looked back at Robbie and put his finger over his mouth to indicate mystery.

"Ah my friend, this is my dear old, old friend."

He laughed very loud which caught the attention of Natasha who started walking towards him with open arms.

"Blimey, if that's old then I'll be a monkey's uncle," murmured Robbie to himself.

Out of the corner of his eye he just caught the reflection of the white telecom van which had been at the hotel. He jotted down its registration number and made a quick phone call.

Negotiations

The nine o'clock meeting of the Cigar Club was quite brief. All the bids were analysed for return and for possible future deals. The bidders were not only offering money. There were some veiled threats and hints of retribution if the deal was not solely theirs.

The Cigar Club members weighed up the pros and cons and risks of doing business with each offer. In particular, the Arab bid was the roughest approach, obviously by people with not much experience in diplomacy and deal-making. Some of their threats were bordering on terrorist talk amid religious quotes and examples of what could happen.

They were dismissed in an instant and preparations were made with their military and intelligence contacts to find out just who they were dealing with.

After tense negotiations there was only one buyer prepared to go as high as one and a half million dollars. A phone call was made.

At ten o'clock, Madame Jin's dark blue Bentley stopped at the King's Club entrance and the car door was opened by the chauffeur.

They were not going in however, as women are not allowed at the King's Club. Instead, a tall, smart gentleman carrying an umbrella and an A3-size yellow envelope got into the car. It drove off briskly into the light traffic.

"Good afternoon, everyone, I am Sir Rodney Applegate, or more formally Lord Aspen . . . but Sir Rodney will do if you don't mind."

The Chinese man bowed gently and Jin Shi Tian introduced her superior.

"You know me as Tian, Sir Rodney from our previous discussions, but may I introduce my senior negotiator and embassy diplomat Tan Ming Jie who will be the one actually handling the sale of your . . . 'latest book'."

"Very pleased to meet you sir and thank you Tian for being so prompt with your attendance – and in such a beautiful car. I have the same model myself."

Jie looked at Sir Rodney, bowed slightly and smiled.

"Yes, it is the best of British design and heritage . . . and now built by German engineers I'm told."

"Quite, quite, yes, we often joke that it is the deluxe model of the Volkswagen Beetle you know. And our similarly grand Rolls Royce is now owned by BMW. What a topsy-turvy world we live in Mister Tan. It is all about power and money in the end. Who can buy what and who can sell valuable commodities to the highest bidder," replied Sir Rodney.

With that, Sir Rodney quickly checked his mobile phone to ensure that the money had been transferred to his private Swiss bank account. He nodded and grunted agreement, then handed over the envelope to Mister Tan.

"Everything is in place Mister Tan and I thank you for your business."

Mister Tan looked at Tian and said something abrupt in Chinese to her. Tian nodded and turned to Sir Rodney with a smile.

"Mister Tan says that he hopes the information is worth paying all that money . . . and that he hopes you have some more . . . specific project information for him next time."

As the Bentley was arriving back at the entrance to the King's Club after circling around the busy Kensington block, Sir Rodney shook Mister Tan's hand.

"We are in the process of securing such information as we speak and I will keep you informed as to what it is and an amount that it may be worth. I don't know how high you may go without higher approval Mister Tan . . . but this one will be in a class of its own."

Mister Tan again said something to Tian.

"Mister Tan say, take your time to assess who your business friends are . . . and don't change boat mid-stream or go Russian about, Sir Rodney."

Tian and Sir Rodney nodded slowly to each other, wary that Mister Tan was now looking straight ahead with a distinct lack of emotion.

The chauffeur had opened the car door and was waiting for their guest to get out. Sir Rodney never looked back as he re-entered the King's Club, thinking about the cool one and a half million-dollar payday.

Inside the Bentley, Mister Tan was taking a quick look at the documents from the yellow folder. A scanner device was lowered from the back of the front seat. Mister Tan handed the documents one at a time to Tian who processed them through the scanner, which were immediately transmitted to their local embassy in London.

As they drove through Kensington on their way back to the embassy, Tian received a phone call.

There was a lot of shouting going on from the caller and poor Tian was fraught with fear and anger. Passing the phone to Mister Tan, Tian bowed her head in shame.

Mister Tan listened to the now quiet but stern voice at the other end for only a few seconds before terminating the call, still looking coldly straight ahead. Not another word was spoken for the remainder of the journey back to the embassy.

They had bought some useless information but more significantly had also created an investigative trail between their operations centre and the now exposed Cigar Club.

There was never any doubt that the money would be returned in exchange for keeping quiet about what had transpired.

Regardless of whether the Cigar Club could maintain their position within the hallowed halls of wealthy aristocrats, their deathly quietness would be on the minds of many individuals.

Mister Tan had lost face with his superiors. He would also be ridiculed by rival foreign agencies for not taking due care of the proceedings and of his choice of field agent, Jin Shi Tian.

Mister Scarab

Kasparov had missed out on the Cigar Club offerings which was an incredible stroke of luck. His people got word that the information hack was just an MI6 setup to flush 'players' out of their foreign hide-outs.

Agents were always changing location or title or usefulness in such a busy place as London. After all, it is the financial capital of the world regardless of what the Americans or Swiss would have you think and it is widely known as a safe haven for doing business between all sorts of factions and people with ideological differences.

He waited outside the Mayfair Mews hotel near the foyer for the hopeful return of Tian, in the event that she wasn't hastily packed off home to face the mandatory intense interrogation.

One and a half million dollars can buy a lot of noodles he thought with a grin.

Sure enough, the sign on a city taxi was sufficient evidence to indicate that Tian had at least survived being bundled onto a private jet, with time enough to pack her things before being sent home for 'retraining'.

Tian got out of the taxi which had stopped outside her suite and waited for the other passenger to get out. He was a sharply dressed Chinese man with sunglasses and ear-piece,.

He looked around in keeping with his minder duties and stared at Tian with an urgency bordering on military discipline. He waited at her door whilst she quickly packed.

The taxi driver was anxiously waiting for their return trip. It was then that Kasparov noticed that the driver was also Chinese.

The minder almost stood to attention as he received orders through his ear-piece and swung around to issue some brief command to Tian before jumping back into the taxi, which then drove away at a fast pace.

Kasparov walked up to Tian's suite door observing her sitting on the bed with a distraught look.

She immediately looked up at Kasparov and became defensive.

"What are you doing here? This is not a good time to be visiting me, especially if you are here to gloat!"

Kasparov smiled but remained at the doorway.

"Ah Tian, I know how you must feel my dear. If it wasn't for the fact that you people seem to have more money than sense, then it would be me who would be packing. I hope that common sense prevails and that you do not get the blame. How are we to know what was in those papers?"

Tian looked at the apparently sincere Kasparov and shook her head.

"Our people do not like to lose face Mister Kasparov. It is in our culture and we must exact revenge for what has taken place."

"But who is to blame when it was that Davis who has baited everyone . . . and the Cigar Club greed to make a quick sale demonstrates their apparent lack of knowledge about what they were indeed selling and where the information had originated," replied Kasparov, slowly entering the room.

Tian thought through the argument.

"We are both exposed, just as the Cigar Club has blown its cover. If nothing else, MI6 has now breached the security leak at the DRI plant. We may as well go home," she said sadly.

"What, no more fish and chips, bangers and mash and that apologetic mannerism of the English that makes everything so nice and self-sacrificing?" said Kasparov with hands outstretched.

They both laughed.

Kasparov noticed Ruby riding her bicycle up to the front entrance and turned to Tian, pointing to where Ruby was now standing.

"Ah, young love. I can feel it in that girl Tian. This is what we should be doing instead of all this spying and negotiating and espionage. Oh, where have all the years gone when I could ride my bicycle and call on my beautiful young girlfriend?"

Tian smiled and relaxed, thinking about what a teenage Kasparov would have been like before all his training, conditioning and harrowing experiences.

"Maybe we can have that meal at the restaurant before we both return to our homelands. What do you say Tian? We are no threat to each other anyway," asked Kasparov sheepishly.

Tian removed two guns and then a knife from under her tunic and put them into the diplomatic bag. Ilya was unmoved except for nodding his head in approval at the weaponry . . . including her smooth long legs . . . his weapon of choice.

"Well, we did have to skip out on what could have been an interesting dinner Ilya. I have been given just this night at the hotel before going to the airport."

"Ah, will you be getting the Bentley again or our dear friend Robbie's taxi?" asked Kasparov sarcastically.

"Oh, I don't think I'll be riding in a Bentley for quite a while."

"You know, I have never ridden in a Bentley . . . or a Rolls . . . or even the Porsche, Maserati or Lamborghini sports cars. We tend to go for taxis and walking . . . oh and catching the bus, tram and train," goaded Kasparov.

They both laughed as Kasparov left the room.

"So sorry, will seven o'clock be a good time Tian?"

"That will be perfect. Thank you Ilya. Now I must shower and change."

Kasparov glanced back at Tian in a different light, allowing his mind to wander . . . and wonder.

Tian just smiled softly, shaking her head in amusement.

No sooner than Kasparov had entered his own suite and placed the key-tag into the internal service slot, a speeding car was heard to drive away fast down the road, squealing its tyres as it rounded the bend.

As he rushed to open the door, he could hear Milly shouting and screaming at the foyer entrance. Tian was also making her way to see what was going on, carefully hiding a gun back into her tunic.

Both Kasparov and Tian arrived at the foyer at the same time and tried to calm down the hysterical Milly. Ruby's bicycle was lying on the ground. One wheel had been run over and was severely buckled.

"She's gone. They've taken her. They pulled her into the car," cried out Milly, visibly shaking and falling to the floor.

"Who has taken who Milly? Is it Ruby you are talking about?" asked Kasparov.

Tian crouched down next to her and put her arm around her.

"What has happened Milly. Calm down and tell us exactly what happened. Everything. Every little detail," demanded Tian calmly.

Milly quietened down and slowly revealed what she had seen.

"Ruby was coming over to see me just now. She came on her bicycle. I heard the front door start to open and then these two men . . . two men grabbed her and pushed her into a car that was outside. I don't know what they'll do with her. She is such a sweet girl."

Tian knew that immediate action was required to get Ruby back as soon as possible.

"What did the car look like and how would you describe the men?" asked Tian slowly.

Milly composed herself and concentrated on what she had seen.

"Blue . . . the car was blue. I'm sure I saw it yesterday too. It had the four circles on the back, like Olympic rings."

"That would be an Audi," said Kasparov, "And the men, what can you tell us about the way they looked."

Milly winced and was trying hard to think about the men.

"They looked like Middle-Eastern men I think or somewhere in that area . . . they had short beards and were wearing sunglasses . . . oh I'm so worried about Ruby."

"Tian, you wait here for the police to arrive and I'll see what I can do to help," said Kasparov as he rushed out of the door.

"Robbie . . . I must contact Robbie and also Ruby's parents, but first the police," said Milly.

Tian helped her up and they made their way to the foyer and the reception telephone.

As Milly made her call to the Police, Tian used her radio to let her people know what had happened and if they could help.

The Chinese embassy certainly knew about Roger Davis and his loose association with both Eric and Ruby, albeit as temporary bit-part players, collecting minor information about the hotel guests.

Whilst waiting for the police to arrive, Milly phoned Robbie. He was waiting at the airport in the taxi ring, talking with fellow cabbies about the ways of passengers and tall tales about their strange requests.

Robbie was shocked and immediately drove off the rank to head home, trying to call Ruby's father, Harry Peters as he drove well over the speed limit. He was put on message bank and left a short message to contact him. Immediately he sent a group SMS message to his mates who meet yearly in Scotland.

Harry Peters returned the call.

"What's up Robbie. Do you want any help with anything?"

"Just listen Harry. I'm sorry but Ruby has been snatched from outside the hotel by what looks like some Middle Eastern people and we need to get going on this now."

Harry was in agony and sought to regain his senses.

"Why Robbie? Why would anyone take my Ruby? They'd better not put one finger on her or I'll kill them all. Is it anything to do with the team?"

"I doubt it Harry. That was a long time ago. Meet me at the Mayfair Hotel, Harry and I'm also waiting on our team to get down here pronto. We need to solve this quick Harry. We need to get Ruby back and deal with those bastards!"

"I'm on my way Robbie."

"The police will have arrived by now and we have some good information to go on already. Apparently, it was a blue Audi. I'll see you soon."

Back at the hotel, the police were questioning Milly and taking measurements outside where the Audi had run over Ruby's bicycle.

A black Range Rover pulled up at speed outside and four men got out flashing security badges at the startled police forensic team.

"Roger Davis, MI6. Give me a quick rundown on what you've got," shouted Davis to the police detective.

"D.I. Osborne sir. Looks like a well-planned abduction so far. The car was seen around here yesterday - a blue Audi, possibly an A6. Occupants are at least two men, Middle Eastern appearance, sunglasses, neat trimmed beards. I would say security, maybe military or mercenaries – but definitely professionals. We have road blocks set up and we are checking the security cameras from outside and along the most likely route to any of their embassies or consulates," replied Osborne.

Davis looked over at Milly who was puzzled at his new appearance.

"Hello Milly, remember me. I gave your son a lift to school the other day. I was undercover with the white van."

"I remember you. You were here fixing the Internet and having breakfast. What's going on then? Why were you here? Have you got anything to do with Ruby's disappearance? She is my Eric's girlfriend you know. I don't know what to say to her mother."

Davis had been found out. He looked at Milly and told her the basic truth of the matter.

"This is not a part of why I was here before Milly. This is another matter entirely, I assure you. I was going to ask Alex and Ruby to let me know when two of your guests were coming and going that's all. This is obviously a different matter and with totally different people."

"Just find her. We'll talk more about the other matter later. You need to be looking for her now," she replied angrily.

"We will get her back Milly. I must go and organise things. D.I. Osborne will keep you informed."

"I'll assign a few men to stay around here for a while too to search the grounds and keep you safe," said Osborne.

Davis ran back to the car, grabbing the keys to drive himself with the other agents in the back.

"I think much better when I'm driving. Sorry guys. We're headed for the Saudi Embassy. That car followed me the other day when I had both Ruby and Alex in the car. They must be holding Ruby to ransom for the information that was sold to the Chinese lady, Tian. They probably now know that I allowed useless information to be hacked in order to flush them out."

"Can we go into the embassy? I mean they do have diplomatic immunity," asked agent Sloane.

"We can wait outside and check that the car went in, first of all. They will not harm her because they know the consequences would be most severe," replied Davis.

Just as Davis was driving past Tian's suite, she held out her hand for them to stop. Davis wound down his window.

"You have done this Davis. You may have flushed out your mole that was leaking hacked documents and also spoiled my cover and that of Kasparov. But it seems you have also severely irritated the Arabs and they may try to take Ruby out of the country," scolded Tian.

Davis was now feeling the heat, but set the record straight.

"It was purely by accident that these Arabs saw me driving with Alex and Ruby and they think that they have some bargaining power with me for her release."

"Now listen here. My people have already determined that the Audi A6 is headed to the wharf area in Liverpool East and you should be looking there. That's all I can do for you, or rather for that nice girl," replied Tian tersely.

"Thanks Tian. I'll get right on it. I was only doing my job you know."

Meanwhile, Robbie was nearing the hotel when he was stopped by Kasparov waiting at the side of the road.

"Can't stop now Ilya, I've got some big problems and the girl down the road has been abducted from our hotel."

"Yes I know. Let me in and I may be able to help you. You are very good people and I also have some very special people who can help," replied Kasparov.

Kasparov jumped into the taxi and explained the bare basics of what he was doing at the hotel.

"I am a negotiator, Robbie. I buy information and equipment for my government which is . . . not always for sale. I think you know what I mean, yes? I only meet people, business people but I have network of intelligence support that may be useful to find the girl, Ruby."

Robbie was shocked. It was certainly an interesting day. Thoughts turned again to Ruby and what she must be going through.

"Have you got anything to do with this Ilya? Have you led these people to my hotel?" shouted Robbie, slowing the car down.

"No, no it has nothing to do with my business, I assure you. But I think that your government has leaked information to a third party and your government agent called Davis took Eric and Ruby to school in his van. I think they assume that they have some bargaining power over him."

Robbie thought for a while.

"A white van? I've seen it hanging around. I thought it had something to do with our Internet problems until it followed us to the airport yesterday," replied Robbie angrily.

Kasparov looked at Robbie.

"Your agent was doing surveillance on your guests at the hotel in case they were doing something wrong. This is quite normal and expected with foreign business people . . . but another matter has been misinterpreted by these Arabs. They are looking to make some easy money. Ruby should be quite safe."

Robbie was thinking way beyond Kasparov's analysis of the situation.

"And what if they can't get their information . . . what then?" he asked, putting his foot down to the floor.

"I thought these days were over," continued Robbie quietly.

As they approached the hotel, Davis' car passed them by. An alert Kasparov knew it was Davis. An agitated Davis was unsure whether he had seen Kasparov in Robbie's taxi.

Kasparov received a message from his people through his earpiece and thought about whether to tell Robbie.

"I have some of my mates arriving here soon, including Ruby's father, Harry. They will be very handy should any force be needed to secure Ruby's return," said Robbie.

"And who are they? It will be very dangerous my friend. No place for amateurs. These people will be armed with guns, explosives," replied Kasparov inquisitively.

Robbie looked at Kasparov with the look only an ex-soldier can give to a pen-pusher masquerading as a spy.

He rolled up his sleeve.

"French Foreign Legion . . . thirty years ago my friend, on a five-year contract. Some of my buddies were in for longer . . . some are dead. They are highly skilled in different areas of soldiering and are afraid of nothing."

Kasparov was both impressed and surprised at seeing the words 'Honour and Fidelity' in green and red on his left arm, yet decided not to tell Robbie that he was an ex-Major in the Russian army and retained the title for his intelligence work.

"Then I shall tell you that the car is headed for the wharf area in the port of Liverpool East. We have it on satellite already. I will keep you informed . . . you and your army my friend. The ring leader has been identified as Mister Scarab."

"Scarab the Arab . . . get outa here!" replied Robbie.

They laughed loudly, but it was soon back to business.

"Does your wife know about your past life," asked Kasparov quietly.

"No. She thinks we are a fishing club that travels to Scotland every year for the salmon."

After a pause . . . they both smiled before focussing back on the job at hand.

"Let's go fishing Ilya."

Back at the Mayfair Mews hotel a young man was approaching with both apprehension and excitement.

Eric could see police forensics combing over the front foyer area and . . . what was that on the ground, covered with tape and paint?

It was Ruby's bicycle!

He raced into the foyer where his mother was still shaking and upset. Ruby's mother was sitting quietly in a chair surrounded by two police women monitoring her emotional state. She seemed catatonic.

"What's happened Mum . . . is it Ruby? Where's Ruby? Where is she?

As Milly explained what had happened, Eric became increasingly pale and he started to think about the roles they had been playing to help Davis monitor two of their guests. Except it wasn't play at all. It was now very serious and Ruby was in great danger.

"Eric, Eric, please I want to have a word with you."

It was Tian. This surprised Eric but he had heard the abductors were of Middle Eastern appearance, so he felt no anger towards her.

"Eric, I know that you and Ruby were collecting information on Mr Kasparov and me for that Roger Davis . . . but this is not part of that at all. These are Arab terrorists who will probably want to exchange Ruby for information that they could not steal or buy. She is safe for the moment."

Eric looked at her with tears in his eyes.

"I can't lose Ruby. I just can't. Where have they taken her?"

"Leave it up to the professionals Eric. Roger Davis, Mr Kasparov and my own team are all trying to get her back. She is an innocent bystander in all this and we will all do our best to rescue her. We have tracked the car down to the wharf in Liverpool East and we will soon surround the area."

Eric was thinking quickly and erratically, unable to sit around and do nothing. He remembered the Mercedes parked at the rear of the building and though he didn't have a licence, he could drive reasonably well.

He reasoned that too many people were involved in Ruby's rescue. Ruby was at a greater risk because of this.

"I'm going there now to rescue her myself," blurted Eric, running to the garage for the car keys, "there are too many people involved, too much activity and mistakes will be made. I need to find her first."

After starting the car, he drove it slowly around to the exit road so as not to attract the attention of the police.

Realising that Eric was going to the search area regardless of any consequence and with his total lack of experience, Tian opened the passenger door and jumped in.

It would seem that the entire world was looking to rescue Ruby.

'Diamond' had now finished playing silly games.

He was also sitting next to one of China's best remote combatants, known to foreign powers as 'Taipan'.

Women and Boats

Ruby was feeling quite bruised after being pushed into the Audi by the Arabic men who looked as though they meant business.

They only spoke in Arabic to each other and would occasionally look at her or grab her chin roughly to enforce their power over her.

Ruby's survival skills kicked in early as she decided to go with the flow but would escape given the first chance. She maintained a strong but compliant attitude and always looked straight ahead and not directly at them.

She also resolved to fight for her life should there be any untoward physical interference to her by these men and would never allow herself to be drugged or tied up.

The men themselves were quite anxious and looked as though they were waiting for further instructions.

The blue Audi stopped at one of the wharf entrances and Ruby was ushered out of the car and pulled quickly along the jetty towards a fishing boat by the man she now assumed was the leader of the two. She could see the other man quickly removing the plates from the Audi then throwing them into the water.

The fishing boat seemed to be about forty feet long and had a mast and boom with enclosed sails. There were other fishing boats along the jetty, some in front and some behind. There was no activity at all, making it futile to scream for help.

She didn't feel much like a 'Scarlett' now and vowed to choose a more intelligent way of life once she graduated . . . if she ever had that chance.

The man pushed her onto the boat and through the turret cabin towards some steps.

"Get down there and keep quiet! You will find something to eat and drink and maybe you want to have a sleep. If you make any trouble for us . . . we will kill you. Make no mistake about that."

Ruby nodded and headed down the steps.

"Where are you taking me?" she asked hesitantly.

The man looked at her and saw through her bravado.

"You are safe if you keep quiet. When we are paid you will be released unharmed. Hopefully this will not take long. What is your name?"

"Ruby, my name is Ruby."

"Well Ruby, I hope for all our sakes that the money will be paid soon. I wouldn't want to have to sell you to my dealer friends."

She continued down the steps and found the cabin door was unlocked. She entered the cabin and locked the door from the inside then went over to the bed to sit down, now all alone and afraid of what could happen to her if things went wrong.

She removed the hair-tie that Eric had given her a few days ago, holding it closely, thinking of her parents, her boyfriend Eric and the state of her predicament.

Eric had told her that the present was to keep them close forever and that he would always be near to her as long as she wore it.

He said there would be a riddle to solve about the hair-tie which was like no other and that he would tell her on the weekend.

She looked at it closely, turned over to the back and looked at a small plastic irregularity.

"Wait a minute, what's this then?" she whispered.

There was a small button-switch!

She pushed it and a miniature LED started flashing.

"No way you super-nerd! Is this a tracking beacon or what?" she gushed quietly.

She was not aware just how close Eric was in fact. Not far away at all, as Eric and Tian were finally approaching the Liverpool wharf area.

It was beginning to look like a family barbecue as 'everyone' was there, keeping quiet, observing various parts of the wharf, looking out for the blue Audi.

Davis was there with a contingent of MI6; Kasparov and Robbie were there talking the rest of the ex-Legionnaires into their search positions; the police were liaising with Port Control and Customs; and there was the approaching Scarab who wanted to see his bait before asking for a substantial payment for her release.

Robbie's mate, another ex-Legionnaire, Dave Brent had organised for the union wharf workers to scour the area and report to him if they saw anything suspicious.

Eric and Tian merely complemented this most unusual gathering.

Eric was alerted to a beeping sound coming from his belt! It was a low frequency sound beeping at around once every two seconds.

Tian looked at a surprised Eric who was just beginning to understand what was happening.

"She's activated it! Ruby has worked out that my present to her was a homing device, all on her own . . . without the riddle or anything! I didn't even know she was wearing it yet!"

Tian nodded to Eric and smiled widely.

"You may have just saved her life Eric . . . just by being in love. What a fortunate present to give to her, although a bit whacky I must say. A nice bracelet would have been another good choice."

"I thought it was in keeping with our forage into the world of spying . . . but now I wish that my quest for excitement had not got us into so much trouble. The days of 'Diamond' will end when we get her back."

"Diamond? Is that the name you have chosen for yourself?" she asked with a laugh.

Eric screwed up his nose and nodded embarrassingly.

"Yeah, supposedly like a hard stone, polished and refined . . . with a high value and multi-faceted perspective."

"And does Ruby also have a secret operative name?"

Eric laughed, looking at Tian. As if a girl could have any suitably fitting name for a spy he thought to himself.

"She goes by the name of . . . 'Scarlett'."

Before he had a chance to pull it to pieces, Tian looked at him sternly down her nose to jolt his perception of women spies . . . in fact of her own persona.

"My name is 'Taipan'. But it was not named by me . . . rather by my reputation for the number of hits I have completed . . . and by the way I stalk and kill my unsuspecting prey," she said in a most sinister tone, poking Eric in the rib cage.

He read once that this is how Chinese agents kill their enemies . . . a quick light jab to the liver area, then in one hour it ruptures totally, spewing black clotted blood out of the victim's mouth, apparently with no medical procedure available to stop them dying.

Eric swallowed and closed his eyes momentarily.

"Taipan is good. Yes, I think Taipan works for me."

Tian settled back in her seat and stretched her arms and arched her back like a contented cat.

Eric caught the outline of a gun, nestled just below her armpit.

"Let us find Ruby before everyone else gets in the way Eric."

The beeper was now emitting a higher frequency at a faster pulse rate. Eric manoeuvred the Mercedes around buildings and down lane ways to improve the distance between them and Ruby according to his radio receiver.

Robbie was in one of the buildings that they passed. The Mercedes only had its parking lights on causing many people to keep watching where it was going.

"I've got one just like that parked behind the hotel Ilya. I used it to take Eric and Ruby to their dinner at the restaurant the other day. Wouldn't mind one myself."

Kasparov entered the registration into his phone 'app' and within five seconds he came up with the owner and address.

"Joseph Finch, 14 Redmond Street . . ." started Kasparov.

"Dogbol!" they both shouted together.

"That's been nicked from the back of my house. They've pinched my . . . Eric! Eric must have taken the Mercedes to look for Ruby!" continued Robbie.

Kasparov thought quickly.

"Everyone needs to be told that your son Eric is here Robbie or he may be mistaken for a terrorist."

The Mercedes continued on its zigzag pathway down to the wharf entrance, where near the end of the jetty, Ruby was trapped inside, held captive by the Arabs.

"Look, there's the blue Audi," shouted Tian.

They pulled over and surveyed the scene. There was one man of Arab appearance coming up on the deck of a boat a mere one hundred yards away. Then another! They must have heard the Mercedes pull up and were looking for signs of movement.

Satisfied that they were merely jumpy and now getting tired, the men went down below again.

Tian retrieved two guns from her tunic, deciding to use the Beretta Bobcat 22. She had only turned around for a few seconds and as she looked for Eric, he could be seen sneaking up towards the boat.

Tian made a call to her people for backup.

Eric crawled up to the boat and reached over the side to get a better hold for climbing aboard. A rope with a metal clasp fell onto the deck.

Eric hid himself from the view of the step-well.

One of the men emerged slowly with a gun, from the step-well and cabin. Looking around, he analysed all the likely places that someone could gain access to the boat. Then he saw something. It was Eric's pale skinny hand grasping the side.

The man approached, this time with a knife, with the obvious intention of silencing the intruder. He raised the knife and looked over the edge. Eric had his eyes closed.

There were sounds like two slight thuds and Eric felt the full weight of the man . . . then the warmth of his sticky blood, spurting over his face and shirt. There was no time for fear.

Eric pushed him away and quickly positioned the body so that it could not be seen from the wheel-house door. He looked for Tian but couldn't see her standing on the deck of the boat behind him, training her gun on the hatch leading to the stairs.

Eric could hear the other man talking and also Ruby's voice. Yes, it was his Ruby, still alive and now arguing with the other man on the boat. Then the sound of a door being smashed open, followed by Ruby yelling out for the man to stop touching her. The next thing, the man was screaming in Arabic and he could hear footsteps running up the stairwell.

Ruby had given the man a few lessons in karate – but he had recovered in an instant. The stakes were high.

"Ruby, Ruby . . . over here he whispered to her."

"Help me, Eric! He has a gun and a knife and he is coming up the stairs . . . run, run!"

Ruby grabbed Eric's' bloody hand and together they threw themselves off the boat onto the edge of the jetty with a two foot rim to hide behind. But they decided to run for it.

The angry man emerged from the wheel-house and was as mad as hell that his captive had escaped. He pointed his gun at arm's length at shadows and shapes until he made out the outline of Eric and Ruby running up the jetty to its end.

Tian swung into action and put two bullets into the man's torso and head. As he was crumpling to the ground, he let off one shot which hit Tian in the shoulder. She fell and hit her head on the deck of the boat.

Suddenly, a drone mysteriously floated overhead with an attached under-belly camera. It picked up on the dead Arab who had fallen in the boat and using biometrics the control station was able to identify his mangled body. One bullet had gone right through his head, straight between his eyes, blowing a bigger hole on its exit at the back of his head.

The drone then surveyed the unconscious Tian who was alive but out of action. Another quick analysis showed that the famous 'Taipan' had been caught in the midst of a deal with the Arabs.

A motorbike arrived. The drone image obtained through the helmet visor showed that 'Scarab' himself was part of the plan and had arrived to finalise the deal.

Back at base, the American remote drone team had brought to an end their six-month surveillance of the suspicious boat which had arrived from Tripoli.

All around, the other observers were unsure at first who the drone belonged to, and why they had no prior knowledge of the deal that was going down . . . and quite badly by the look of it.

Back at the US drone base, a dilemma was taking place.

"What do you want to do Jack? We can sink the boat once Scarab gets on board and let the Brits tidy up, or we can go in there. There's too much activity going on. Christ's sake . . . everyone's there and we nearly missed our chance," said Jed Cooper.

"Where is Scarab now?" asked Jack.

"He just got on the boat and is heading down the wheel-house steps."

Jack looked at Cooper and gave the final order for the operation.

"Fire in the hole Jed. Make it quick and get our drone outa there fast."

Jed brought the drone back into the area of the boat and placed it at the wheel-house entrance. There was a click and thump as the drone containing a charge of plastic explosives tumbled down the steps towards the trapped Scarab.

There was a tremendous explosion as the boat exploded, sending debris flying over the head of Tian who was just gaining consciousness.

All of a sudden, the area was swamped with agencies and departments, along with Kasparov and Robbie and his mates.

Sirens were wailing and the Port emergency vehicles were put into action. Everyone had to stay back near the wharf because of the intense heat and flames.

Harry Peters and Robbie Johnson looked at the grim scene and broke down in despair at what they thought was the demise of Ruby and Eric amid possible throwbacks to their days in the Legion.

Davis was another stunned observer who looked on in horror at what he considered was the gravest mistake of his life. How could he have used mere children to do his field work involving foreign agents?

Then he saw Tian lifting herself up from the boat next the one that had blown up. Her coat was on fire.

Before Davis could act, Kasparov leaped onto the boat and put out the flames on her coat, noticing that she had a severe wound to her shoulder as she cried out in pain. He summoned the medics but was quickly pushed out of the way by two Chinese men who carried her away quickly to a waiting car.

It was a dark blue Bentley.

The old Chinese gent that he had seen previously was staring at Kasparov through the open window, devoid of any emotion.

Fire crews were arriving to put out the fires and it was Harry Peters who had the first words to say.

> "I have to know if she was on that boat . . . and if she was, who these bastards are . . . who they work for . . . and who blew up the boat to hide the evidence."

> "I'm with you Harry," said Robbie, "but we have to be certain and we have to have closure on all this . . . even if it takes me a lifetime to work out who was to blame. And I also want to know who was operating that drone."

The area was now being sealed off for the forensic team to analyse every fragment of material that was in and around the boat. Divers were called in. Phone calls were made. MI6 was in control of the situation.

The mood was indeed sombre and one would expect that the only thing left for Davis to do for the moment was to arrest the Cigar Club members and analyse the implications of how so many foreign agents acting against the British Government were in the one place at the same time, without the prior knowledge of MI6 or GCHQ.

However, this was not the end of it all, as we know that Eric and Ruby were last seen running towards the end of the jetty.

It would not be long before forensics would discover that Eric and Ruby did not perish in the blaze.

But where were they? Were they alive, or at the bottom depths of the murky oily water, beneath the sunken boats?

Phoenix Pair

Eric and Ruby were indeed lucky even if they didn't think so at this time, for just before the gunfire battle with Tian and the boat blowing up into a fiery grave, they had leapt wildly over the jetty edge onto another boat.

It was the very last boat on the same jetty. They stumbled into the forward cabin, down below deck, locked the door and barricaded the doorway with the bed.

Ruby was trapped again . . . but this time with Eric.

They had heard and felt the explosion but being unable to see anything could not assume that all was right for them to surface.

They were tired. They were afraid. It was then that Ruby realised that Eric was covered with blood and who knows what else from the Arab terrorist.

Eric managed to clean himself up and found some dry clothes in one of the cupboards. They were big, but they were clean and didn't smell too bad.

Ruby also managed to freshen up before flopping down on the bed to sleep. Eric stood guard nervously at the locked door with a piece of metal pipe.

At about four o'clock in the morning, Eric was feeling quite dozy but was suddenly alerted to the movement of feet on their boat. He reasoned that two men had come aboard and were talking in the wheel-house. They were Americans.

Ruby had woken up and was also listening to the voices.

"Looks like we can get out of here now Ruby. I'll go up first and check them out. They must have had the security clearance to get past all that must be going on up there."

Ruby reached for his arm and signed for him to be quiet.

"This is a very seedy part of town Eric, so let's listen for a bit to see just who they are. This is England. They are foreigners."

They didn't have to wait long.

"Good thing we had the right security to get through Joe or else we would never get those stones out tonight," said one of the men.

"Yeah Jay, lucky that our guys took out that boat with Scarab and his cronies on board, eh? The Brits can clean up for us and we can just sail away with the diamonds to get our money owed. No trail to implicate us at all," replied the other.

"They should be down below according to our briefing, surrounded by cans of food," replied Jay.

"Better check I suppose," said Joe as he moved to descend the stairs to the forward cabin.

Jay looked surprised that Joe was going to be anywhere near the diamonds – their diamonds.

Eric raised his pipe and thought about Ruby's safety.

The American tried the locked door a few times and decided that that's how it was supposed to be – in case they ran off with the goods before delivery. He went back up to the wheel-house.

"The door's locked and we don't have no key, so I suppose we gotta wait until we reach Amsterdam tomorrow."

"Nobody trusts nobody anymore Joe. You know that," murmured Jay, now more relieved.

They both laughed aloud before the roar of the engine coming to life drowned out any further chance of hearing what they were saying.

A few minutes later the boat started moving from side to side and then it felt like it was under way.

Eric and Ruby held each other close at the door to the cabin.

"It's not over yet Eric. These guys seem just as bad as the last lot . . . and we're on our way to Amsterdam!"

Eric was in a state of heightened alert.

"Diamond smugglers. How ironic. We must find a way out before they open the door in Amsterdam because they will not want any witnesses to their crime," reasoned Eric.

"We have about eight hours then. So . . . let's have a look around for the diamonds," offered Ruby, "We may as well see what all the fuss is about . . . things can't get any worse."

Eric wasn't so sure and felt sick about the whole plan, if it was a plan at all. Ruby was already looking for the cupboard with the cans of food – and the diamonds, as Eric just flopped down onto the bed to have a doze.

About three hours later Eric woke up in a sweat. The engines were still rumbling through the hull of the boat and nothing much had changed.

That is until he saw Ruby at the small table, wide-eyed and mesmerised by the glint of diamonds – hundreds of shiny, sparkling diamonds – and they looked pretty big too.

Eric put his arm on her shoulder and gazed at the size and number of expertly cut diamonds. He reasoned they were professionally cut because he knew the penalty for cutting any large stone badly affected the price dramatically. Sometimes they could render a white, perfect diamond worthless. He had gained his expert knowledge from watching 'To Catch A Thief' on TV.

"Look at these Eric. This is a lot of money's worth tied up here. I would say we have a few million pounds worth of rock candy here. Size and cut are equally important. Then there's clarity and colour."

Eric was stunned at how calm she was, absorbed in the world of spies, smuggling, espionage and international crime.

"Where do you get all that from Ruby? Rock candy? I mean, well, we are about to die in about eight hours and your eyes have been replaced with huge diamonds."

Ruby looked a bit sheepish before regaining her composure.

"I worked in a jeweller's shop during my holidays once and I know the four C's well indeed. Well, we may as well have something to bargain with Eric. There is nothing else. We are trapped and there's only one way out . . . or is there?"

Eric looked puzzled and regretted his intrusion into her daydreams.

Ruby thought about the forward cabin layout. It had water pipes and air vents and possibly some forward entrance to where the anchor chain is stored.

She knew that from the time she went with her dad to Scotland to go fishing on his friend's trawler. Moving to the far wall of the cabin, Ruby started tapping on the exterior walls.

"So, we are on a wooden boat for starters. That's handy to know. We are at the pointy end by the way and close to the place where the anchor chain and rope is stored."

Ruby sounded like quite an expert.

"That's the bow I think, Captain Scarlett. Now if I may make a suggestion here. What about smashing through that wall and getting into that chain locker, so that we can hopefully see where we are going . . . of course mindful that the Americans will be looking straight over our heads if we do pop up."

Ruby smiled at Eric then punched him in the chest.

"Not if we pop up during the night time Diamond."

Eric thought it was a hard punch and held his chest until he realised that Ruby could have punched him much harder in the throat or kicked him in his now much-bruised shin in a real fight.

They could hear some loud scraping and banging going on above deck as if they were moving something. Then there was a big splash which indicated they had thrown something quite big into the water.

"That will be the dinghy being moved from on-deck into the water so that they can tow it . . . and use it to hand over the diamonds for their reward money," said Eric.

"We must be getting close Eric. Let's try and break through that wall before they meet up with their friends and discover two stowaways with all their diamonds . . . well most of them."

Eric sighed unconvincingly, then started thinking quite logically that they would not miss a few diamonds. There were so many!

They immediately got down to work, prising away the wall coverings and locating panels and more tools to use for the break-out. At one stage they heard the engines slow down and the Americans talking and listening for where the unusual sounds were coming from.

"Must be a loose anchor or something in the hold," shouted Jay.

He was standing right above their heads, on deck. There was no reply. The engine speed increased again.

About an hour later, the engine was put into neutral. The boat came to a stop, apart from movement caused by the rolling of the waves. Eric and Ruby had broken through to the chain locker and were waiting for the right moment to take a look. The fresh air they could feel was exhilarating and refreshing.

"Jay, get in the dinghy and get that registration number changed on both sides. We don't want to get pulled up by customs or border patrol. There's some paint near the door. Here's the new number – HT07004."

Jay was slow to respond, thinking that he would be in a most vulnerable position to be 'let go', clinging to the side of the boat from the dinghy in a medium swell and wind, then realised that it was a necessary action to prevent getting boarded by customs. He got in the dinghy and inched himself forward around the hull in the rough conditions.

"I can't hold the dinghy steady Joe, you're gonna have to help me here. I'll hook up to one of the cleats up front, but you need to hold this rope tight as I move around," shouted Jay.

Joe was not keen on the idea of hanging upside down from the deck to hold the dinghy in place. He could even be pulled into the water by Jay so that he could have the diamonds for himself.

With no choice, Joe got into position. The movement of the boat forced the railing into his ribs and it hurt. He moved below the railing and held on to the boat with his feet wrapped around a cleat.

This was the moment that Eric was waiting for.

"The engine's still idling Ruby. Get in that wheel-house, put it into forward and get those revs up to maximum as quick as you can to get us out of here. I'll take care of our Americans. Get ready. Do it as soon as you see me standing over that man on deck."

Eric eased himself out of the chain locker and carefully made his way to behind the dangling Joe.

Ruby followed and went via the opposite side towards the wheel-house. All was going to plan.

But just as Eric was over the top of Joe, he was seen by Jay.

"Behind you. Look behind you!"

Without a second thought, Eric let fly with his metal pipe straight into Joe's legs until Joe had no hold around the cleat.

He cried out in pain as he fell into the dinghy on top of Jay, knocking him into the water. They were shouting and cursing and getting quieter as they drifted away from the boat by the swell and waves.

Immediately, the sound of the gear change and increasing revs of the engine moved the boat quickly away from the Americans.

Some shots were fired by the injured Joe but with the movement of the water, they were far from effective.

Eric raced into the wheel-house to see Ruby gripping the steering wheel, her eyes scanning ahead to see where she was going, with the first signs of day break appearing through the clearing clouds.

Then she dramatically swung the boat around with fierce determination in her eyes, watching the movement of the compass. She eventually looked at an amazed Eric.

"You got a ticket Diamond? This ain't no free ride for no freeloaders or thieves. Kiss me now or I'll throw you over the side," she screamed between her teeth, like an American gangster in a movie.

Then she smiled at him with raised eyebrows, leaving Eric wondering who the heck she was, this super-girl of his with a range of skills to match . . . Scarlett!

"You saved our lives Eric. You got me out of trouble with the Arabs . . . and now the rogue American spies. We're going home at last. Will you ever take me to dinner again?"

Eric pressed up against her and kissed her neck.

"You saved both our lives Ruby and I love you so much. You gave me the strength to do what I had to do. Me . . . the nerd with a dream of spying."

Ruby took off her hair-tie and gave it back to Eric.

"I don't need this when I have you close by. You make me feel special Eric and now you have saved me from death. I hope we are never apart from each other – unless I'm on a mission of course."

They gave each other a big hug as they laughed but Eric was keeping focussed on getting home. His eyes narrowed.

"It's not over yet Ruby. We have to get home. We can't use the radio yet as it will be intercepted. So we have to navigate our way close to the England coast before I call Davis on my cell phone."

Ruby nodded in agreement.

"I wonder if there's any food on board this boat?" she asked.

"I'll have a steak sandwich and an ice-cold beer thank you . . . first mate," joked Eric unwisely.

He was too slow to fend off the familiar kick to his shin. Yep, same leg alright. Eric decided it was probably a good idea for him to investigate the food situation himself. Maybe he could make her something to calm her down.

Ruby and Eric took turns in piloting the boat on the way back to England. It was not an easy task in reasonably windy conditions with a mild swell, but they held the compass due West, always on the alert for passing ships.

At least the boat had a radar reflector to warn the big ships, although it is the smaller vessel that must give way.

Eric managed to find some food left by the Americans in their rucksacks – beef, cheese and tomato sandwiches and some vacuum flasks of black coffee.

"I made them myself," joked Eric.

They were hungry. Nothing more was said on the matter. The black, sugarless coffee was finished off in one go. Eric decided not to complain about the lack of milk . . . or the horrible BBQ sauce spread over perfectly good beef. Oh yes, and it was most certainly a bit raw!

All eyes were set on finding the English coastline and arriving home to be with family once again. They relaxed and enjoyed the early morning sunshine breaking through a cumulus sky.

They were in for a rude shock!

Give or Take

Eric wondered about who would be monitoring the movement of their boat. After all they were involved now apparently in a rogue CIA operation that was money laundering diamonds for cash . . . and a kidnapping gone wrong for Scarab who was demanding a ransom for Ruby's release from MI6.

Somehow, Eric and Ruby had foiled both plans and were free . . . now with a boat, diamonds and valuable information for the British Intelligence Services.

Eric had befriended Tian from the Chinese Secret Service too, and they had Roger Davis to fall back on at MI6.

They had no idea that Robbie Johnson and Harry Peters, Eric and Ruby's fathers had befriended Ilya Kasparov from the Russian Secret Service. Now he was working with their fathers' old Foreign Legion buddies to help find them.

The problem with having so many operatives and agencies involved is that there is a lot of communications traffic.

Regardless of their location, GCHQ and MI6 were following the progress of the failed diamond transfer – and the diamonds hadn't arrived! They didn't know where they were or where the two CIA agents had gone. A major search was on for the boat.

Similarly, the Americans were none too pleased to lose two rogue agents and millions of dollars in negotiable diamonds.

Eric and Ruby didn't have to wait long for more trouble and it was none of the fore mentioned parties that was now cutting into the path of their boat in another old fishing boat, shouting through a megaphone at them.

"Prepare to be boarded. This is not a game. You have our goods and we will get them any way we can. There's no reason for anyone to get hurt."

Unknown to Eric and Ruby, it was three members of the Cigar Club team. Cartwright had intercepted coded messages from the CIA and sought to acquire the diamonds for themselves.

Eric and Ruby looked at each other.

"Well . . . analysis Diamond? I think they are British and are unrelated to the rogue CIA agents."

"What makes you think that, Scarlett? I mean does it really make any difference who the hell they are? They want the diamonds and that's that!" replied Eric sternly.

Ruby pointed to the horizon and the emerging coastline. She had a mischievous look about her. Eric thought it wise to protect his shin.

"We can now use the cell phone to contact Davis and also use the radio to report our position and get word to the coast guard that we are in danger of being boarded by . . . by pirates!" blurted Ruby in a rush of excitement.

"We are going straight ahead at full speed. They will be behind us and unable to catch up," she continued.

"Pirates? Where the hell are we Ruby? Pirates in the English Channel?" screamed Eric.

Eric knew that her plan was going ahead regardless of what he thought, but what if they played rough in the meantime?

"What if they start shooting . . . guns, machine guns . . . mortars maybe?"

Ruby set the boat at full revs and pointed it at the boat that was coming towards them. She pulled away last minute causing a huge wash to strike their boat causing them to take evasive action which put them further behind.

Eric reached for his cell phone to call Davis while Ruby grabbed the radio microphone and selected the emergency channel.

Ruby was in her element, pushing ahead at full speed, teeth gritted and eyes narrowed, radio in hand, searching the sea for what lay ahead.

Before she had a chance to press the radio talk button, another boat came into view. She waved and shouted at it . . . but it soon became apparent that the two men on deck were pointing guns at their boat . . . at her.

"How's it going with Davis there Eric? We have a bit of a complication here . . . nothing to worry about, but I think the CIA have just arrived to take back their rock candy."

Eric had just got Davis on the phone but with all the commotion and latest bewildering update from Ruby, he didn't know what to say.

"Just keep going Ruby. I don't think that giving up will save our lives. We have witnessed a little bit too much," he blurted out without considering the consequences.

Ruby headed straight for the CIA boat as if to ram them and then pulled away in the last few seconds as she had done previously. One of the men jumped overboard while the other was knocked over by the bow wave.

"Hello, hello . . . is that you Eric? What are you up to? I always knew you would pull through," ushered Davis with relief.

There were cheers in the background at MI6.

"Mister Davis . . . we need your help badly. We are in a fishing boat headed for Hull and have two other fishing boats chasing us . . . they have guns . . . we have their diamonds," shouted Eric in a panic.

"Stay calm Eric. Is Ruby Ok . . . is she with you and unharmed?"

"Yes, she is at present mowing down the two boats at full speed and contacting the Coast Guard on the radio."

There were more cheers in the background.

"We are onto it now Eric. Help will arrive in the next ten minutes, so if you can hold on until then, everything will be fine," said Davis calmly.

"Ok, everything is under control right Ruby?" he asked hesitantly.

Ruby was watching the two boats behind her, both trying to catch up to them. Then shooting began. Lots of it!

But it wasn't at them they were shooting. It was the two boats fighting it out to eliminate each other.

"No one likes to share anything these days," said Ruby shaking her head, "they're only diamonds after all."

"Worth millions," added Eric.

Ruby laughed and checked the compass bearing again.

This time it was Eric with some bad news.

"Ruby, look! Another boat, Port side."

"Where?"

"On your left Captain," he replied with a chuckle.

Yes . . . it was another kick. But this time the other shin. Eric was hurting yet pleased that his bruised shin was given a rest, but he spoke too soon.

"Owww! Ruby you're going to have to stop doing that. That's one of the things that I don't like about your attitude towards me."

"You mean there's more ways! Tell me about it before I do it again!" she shouted back.

Eric concentrated on the third boat that was visiting them.

"Ruby! The other boat coming towards us. Take evasive action."

Ruby again steered the boat towards them and turned at last minute.

The site of Tian the "Taipan" being knocked off her feet by Ruby and her ego was a sight to behold.

"Ruby they are friends. That is Tian the Chinese agent. She has come to rescue us. Pull over!"

Ruby didn't respond.

"Pull over Ruby!"

Ruby turned to Eric and scoured at him.

"Eric, we have millions of dollars' worth of high-quality diamonds on board. Now do you really think that Tian . . . that carpet snake . . . is here for us . . . or the diamonds?"

Just then Eric's phone beeped and Davis was on the other end to reassure them that all was coming along as planned.

"How are you keeping up Eric? Is Ruby still ok? Keep her calm and let her know that we have help on the way. You should see it soon."

"Hurry up with the help. We now have three boats trailing us and we are alone on this old boat. This is becoming a bit much for us! We are trying to get to the coast."

Ruby had calmed down a bit and was regretting the way she spoke to Eric. She looked at him rubbing his shin.

"That was Davis. Apparently, we will see signs of a rescue soon. He asked if you were ok and told me to keep you . . . calm."

Meanwhile the waters around them were exploding with gunfire, aggressive boat manoeuvres and much shouting and posturing. All three boats were running a sea battle like nothing that was seen in a film. This was real. People were dying and one of the boats had been hit with a grenade and was sinking.

Ruby looked at Eric.

"I need you to hold me, Eric. I need you to know that I am only trying to get us through. I promise not to kick you in the shin anymore."

"Or thump me in the chest?" demanded Eric cautiously and quietly.

She gave him a quick kiss and turned to check the compass, now sporting a wide mischievous grin.

The boat was still at maximum revs but that was not going to last long as smoke started to pour out from the engine bay and the engine began to squeal and shudder – coming to a final stop with a bang.

"The engine's seized! We'd better prepare to fend off any of those silly enough to take on the likes of Scarlett and Diamond, mon Capitaine!" offered Eric defiantly, now much more confident.

He also thought unwisely that he had finally tamed the beast, also known as Scarlett . . . his super-girlfriend.

"I'll put the dinghy in the water on their blind side in case we have to escape. It's on a rope and pulley system and there's a motor on the back," said Eric.

They were now prepared to escape by yet another boat – albeit only twelve feet long. Ruby was impressed at his strength and determination to see them survive. Eric returned and glanced at the backpacks left by the CIA agents.

"We may need the handguns that are in the backpacks Ruby. I'll get them. One each and a magazine of bullets."

"Do you even know how to use a handgun, Eric?"

"Probably not as well as you Ruby I would imagine. So where did you get your training then . . . Junior Spy School?"

Ruby waited a few seconds before replying.

"I've already told you Eric that I have been to Scotland on one of my father's 'fishing trips'. One thing I didn't mention was that I became aware that my father's friends were ex-Legionnaires. I found out by intuition but never told my father or my mother. That explains why he taught me how to look after myself I suppose."

"The Foreign Legion? Gees Ruby, you never cease to amaze me! Now we have another fighting force entwined in our international spy marathon. What else?" he asked.

"Well, on one occasion in Scotland they all went for target practice and I was invited under the strict proviso that my mother would never be told. They were very scared about the future. Dad said that at some time, learning how to use a gun could save my life . . . or take it away if I mix with the wrong people. He said that it is not the gun that kills, but the person holding the gun. Personally, I would blame both!"

Eric thought for a moment, deeply, constructing his theory very carefully.

"And my father . . . he goes every year with your dad?"

Ruby nodded and raised her eyebrows.

"Yep! He's one as well. Our dads are very close. Same with the others . . . in fact I bet they are looking for us right now."

Thoughts turned back to the battle that was going on behind them. It was much quieter. All three boats had sustained quite significant damage and one was sinking, but one was moving slowly towards them. It was the Chinese Tian.

As they pulled up alongside, Tian looked at them without emotion, examining the thick smoke coming from the engine bay, working out that it could not be used for their escape.

Then she smiled briefly at Eric.

"Looks like you have scored yourself a warrior my friend . . . and I believe you have some diamonds that belong to us. They are payment for the loss we made trading useless information from your English Cigar Club. Have you heard of them Eric?"

"Only in passing Tian . . . but we don't have any diamonds . . . we are just escaping from the hands of the Arab abductors who took Ruby from outside the Mayfair."

We have been tracking you Eric since you jumped ship at the jetty. What a marvellous escape . . . you do know that I saved your life . . . twice!" she said slowly, holding her shoulder.

Ruby was having none of this idle chatter.

"There are no diamonds here and that's that and we are expecting help very soon. I advise you to back off and get out of here. You have just killed people and sunk one of the boats behind you. Not a very nice thing to do snake lady."

Tian remained expressionless, nodding to one of her crew.

There was a lot of movement below deck. Three men appeared dressed in black and carrying grappling hooks.

"We are coming aboard. You have no weapons; your boat is damaged so it cannot move and these men are trained martial arts experts."

Eric reached down for his gun. Ruby followed suit and smiled back at Tian who looked decidedly angry.

Another command was issued to the men as the boat came closer. Eric pointed the gun at Tian's boat and pulled the trigger. Nothing happened. The safety catch was on.

As Tian sighed and looked closely at Eric, Ruby fired two shots into her boat just below the waterline, then eyed up the dinghy alongside their boat, grabbed a black bag and secretly threw it into the dinghy while Eric wasn't looking.

"We are coming aboard now! Please do not resist or I will have to use force, and you know I will Eric. This is not play. I have been sent to collect the diamonds."

Eric was unsure how to proceed. If they got the diamonds, they would just let them stay on the disabled boat. Ruby had other ideas.

"Eric, if you can get into the dinghy quietly, I will hold off this woman until I have finished what I am doing, OK?" she said softly with a look that Eric had seen many times before.

"And exactly . . . what are you doing? You are standing next to me and whispering in my ear. I can see that having an effect."

All of a sudden, the boat began to tilt, slowly at first, then the back started sinking down in the water.

"What have you done? Where are my diamonds?" screamed Tian, watching the boat slowly sinking.

Ruby smiled and waved at her and said, "Get your diamonds, wherever they are and be very quick about it. The boat is sinking . . . bit of a plumbing mix up down below. Never was much good with bathroom renovations."

Ruby looked at Eric with some urgency.

"Get in the dinghy now! . . . we are going to ride the waves to England."

Eric and Ruby dived into the dinghy. Eric quickly pushed off from their sinking boat and looked at the connections between outboard motor and fuel tank. It was right to go.

He squeezed the fuel bulb and pressed the electric start. It spluttered a bit but there was hope that it would start. Sure enough, the next touch of the starter had it roaring into life.

The sea was quite calm now and land was only about five miles away. They zoomed off at maximum revs, far outpacing what an old fishing boat can do.

Eric looked back to see the Chinese men scrambling below deck in an effort to find the diamonds before the boat sunk.

He could also see Tian glaring at them, receding into the distance, most likely wondering if the diamonds were in the dinghy.

Ruby had the wind in her hair and was calmly taking in the breeze. Eric looked at her – closely. She was almost too quiet.

He looked around the dinghy for anything of use. Suddenly he stopped and focussed in on what he thought was a black rag deposited behind Ruby's back.

Ruby caught his gaze. She started whistling and stretching and yawning. Eric's mind drifted back to the black bag containing the diamonds.

"You didn't . . . no . . . you didn't!"

Ruby laughed.

"We'll have a great future Eric, you and me. No financial worries, no need to work unless we really want to . . . and all the good we could do. Imagine that, Eric!"

Eric had no time to respond as he was alerted to a humming sound.

Eric's hearing was quite acute and he could definitely hear something rumbling, tumbling . . . whirring!

"I hope that helicopter is ours Ruby. This boat doesn't have another dinghy or life-raft . . . or anything really. Davis did say help was coming soon, but you know me, I'm always on the side of caution and have a slight problem with probabilities and chance," said Eric matter-of-factly, now not caring too much about their run of good luck.

Their luck was bound to run out sooner or later.

Eric didn't believe in luck. He knew that combinations and permutations were purely mathematical and random success was a bit of a hit and miss affair . . . like throwing a dart for a bullseye when the dartboard was 100 feet away.

The helicopter came closer. The down-draft blew them around a bit but Eric kept racing for the coast uncertain of who they were. He did know that they were now officially in England's waters.

The side door opened. A Chinese face poked outside briefly. Ropes were dispatched with more men in black ready to descend.

"They like their black outfits, don't they?" shouted Ruby.

"Yes Ruby, they do. Black is the new style in men's t-shirts too. Maybe they all think they are Ninja warriors," replied Eric shaking his head.

Suddenly the water began bubbling around them. Those helicopters can cause a lot of turbulence . . . but the bubbling now seemed to be in front of them.

Ruby looked back to where the Chinese boat had been. On the horizon was a British Destroyer steaming towards them.

The helicopter crew hauled in the ropes, closed the doors and zoomed off quickly towards the centre of the English Channel . . . heading for international waters.

Eric dropped the revs on the outboard motor and noticed the bubbling was still in front of the dinghy.

To their amazement, a British submarine broke the surface. Immediately the conning tower hatch spewed out at least five armed-men, searching the area for any danger to Eric and Ruby.

Then coming at fast speed, two Royal Navy helicopters flew past them, heading to where the gun battle had taken place.

The men from the submarine waved and cheered for them.

"You are safe now. We will wait until the pilot boat from Hull arrives. I can see it now coming out of the bay. They'll look after you and I believe your dads are waiting on board to take you home," shouted the leading seaman.

Eric and Ruby had come through the biggest test of their lives and Eric was a changed man.

Ruby was . . . well Ruby was Ruby. Misunderstood by some until you get to know her . . . and then you never really do . . . a paradox of human strength and courage and stubbornness.

The pilot boat arrival was an emotional moment for Eric and Ruby and their dads, although Eric was sort of numbed against the background of their life and death encounters – each moment had been on the edge of a knife.

Ruby understood what her dad had been through and now felt closer to him than ever before. He had merely nodded at her with respect to acknowledge that she had learnt some valuable lessons, holding back his soldier emotions for a quieter moment as he gently hugged her.

When the pilot boat got back to port, the other ex-Legionnaires gathered around them both and gave three cheers.

Davis was also there, in the distance, admiring their courage and his own folly. He looked on at the celebrations and thought about his unchangeable life. At least there was time for these two to reassess their spying aspirations.

Behind the trees at the reception centre was another introspective character . . . Ilya Kasparov, who had got to know Eric's father and had learnt a little more about the struggles of youth . . . for the second time in his life. Davis and Kasparov caught a glimpse of each other. They nodded slowly once in acknowledgement. That was enough display of recognising that their pathways and failings were very similar. They both disappeared into the urban void.

Reunions

Back in the village of Dogbol, Milly Johnson and Carol Peters were waiting for the return of Eric and Ruby who were still going through their debriefing interview with a very unassuming but highly ranked Whitehall administrator. He had no name or title. He was just a bland figure in a suit with a briefcase and digital recorder.

Ruby had managed to keep her black bag with her, telling everyone it was her personal toiletries. Inside indeed were a few containers and jars of various pharmacy products. However, they did not contain much original product.

Strangely enough the explanation worked, although one particular member of the various Government agencies that looked on from behind a two-way mirror had a keen interest in where that bag was going.

"Oh yes, we got . . . most of the diamonds from the boat alright as far as we know. They were hidden amongst tins of food and other rations. We had plenty of time before the boat would have actually sunk . . . and we managed to tow it back to Hull for full forensics," said the interviewer.

"So, there were diamonds then?" exclaimed Ruby.

Eric shook his head, more to show complete amazement at Ruby's gall than that there were actually diamonds found.

"Yes, quite a few. You know you have done quite a lot on your escapades, both of you. You have foiled Ruby's kidnapping, played a part in the demise of your abductors and the demise of Scarab . . . helped to capture two rogue CIA agents and their illegal haul of diamonds . . . oh and have seen off the presence of two foreign agents, Kasparov and that Taipan woman," continued the interviewer.

Ruby thought for a moment about how many boats and attackers there had been in the English Channel skirmishes.

"So, who were the people in the first boat . . . the English ones?" asked Ruby, staring at the two-way mirror with suspicion.

"Yes, the first boat that arrived was an unknown party to all these troubles," added Eric, "and they would have killed us without doubt."

The interviewer looked at the two-way mirror casually and thought that these two knew more than they were letting on. He decided to chance it and name them.

"They were the Cigar Club . . . have you heard of them? Have you ever spoken with any of them? They have high social connections and are known to be very exact in getting what they want," continued the interviewer candidly.

Ruby looked at Eric. Eric looked at the interviewer.

"Tian, the Chinese lady told me that they were the intermediaries for selling British Government information to foreign governments . . . and that she had been duped into buying rubbish for a high price. The ones on the boat who you probably picked up are the only ones that I have seen. I mean . . . I didn't know how they were connected with us before you said just now," reported Eric at length.

The interviewer stood up, excused himself and left the room.

He returned in a minute and sat down, quietly staring at them both. Ruby knew how to outstare anybody, especially Rosemary Winters, alias 'blizzard face' at her school. They were always fighting and staring at each other.

Eric felt very uncomfortable and squirmed in his seat.

"Do you know Roger Davis, Eric? Ruby? . . . He is one of ours and was observing the goings on of Tian and that Russian, Kasparov, in their comings and goings at the Mayfair Mews hotel. So . . . do you know of him . . . our Roger Davis, of MI6," asked the interviewer abruptly but taking care over his choice of words.

Ruby could see what was going on. They were trying to remove Davis as a field agent. The establishment wanted things to stay as they were . . . as they always have been. An upstart like Davis was no match for the 'elite'.

Ruby tried to warn Eric in her response.

"I fail to see how we would know one of your agents except if we met or spoke with him in his undercover guise. We are not prone to playing at spying or other fanciful activities. I'm sure your agent would be most severely compromised if we were to have played any part in his operations . . . whatever they were."

Eric caught on. He could see the dilemma facing Davis. Although approached by Davis, it was Eric and Ruby who had wanted to try out the spying game, invent their own code names and prepare their future for a possible leg-up to some later Government position. It was partly their fault for accepting Davis's approach.

Davis however had made a significant mistake in allowing this to happen . . . and they were still near to . . . well under eighteen and that was not near enough.

The interviewer was no slouch.

"So, you have never worked with, helped out or subsequently been paid by this Roger Davis . . . that you are aware of?"

Ruby stood up.

"We want to go home now whoever you are . . . and I object to you insinuating that we have meddled in any of your agency work or compromised one of your agent's operations."

The interviewer remained calm and spoke softly as if to keep the next question confidential between the three of them.

"Only . . . now I know I'm just an old pen-pusher from Whitehall . . . but there has to be a reason why you were kidnapped Ruby. I mean why were you, out of all the girls in England, selected by these Arabs to be taken forcibly outside the front door of the Mayfair Mews hotel in the middle of the day. Why you do you think that is?"

Eric was thinking fast.

"Well, if I may offer an explanation."

"Yes Eric, let's hear what you have to say on the matter."

Eric stood up and slowly walked around the table, holding his lapel and putting his hand on Ruby's shoulder.

"It seems to me that what I told you about Tian, who I met at the hotel when Ruby was having dinner with me, and what Tian told me after Ruby had been kidnapped, indicate that maybe your agent was the very same person who gave Ruby and me a lift to school after we missed the bus. My mum can back me up on that because she arranged it."

"That's right. So maybe the Arabs, for whatever reason, wanted to blackmail him or extract a ransom from him, then assumed that we were both connected to him . . . maybe even family . . . I suggest," added Ruby, glancing again at the two-way mirror.

The interviewer was stumped. Davis could not be implicated in any misdemeanour or dereliction of duty or ethical code violation.

These two he knew now to be masters of deceit. Not that this was a crime, seeing as he was in the same business on a grander scale and with more resources.

Behind the two-way mirror a certain civil servant named Cartwright made a quick phone call.

"Jeremy, we have no foundation for his removal. He is still on our case. The kids have backed him up. Something needs to be done about the loose ends or we'll not get any more support from our power base."

There was a brief response and then Cartwright flashed his credentials to leave the secure premises.

The interviewer was finished. He smiled at Ruby and showed them the door with a wave of his arm.

"Davis is very fortunate to know you it would seem. Funny, but I thought you would be antiestablishment and authority."

"Oh, we are, we are . . . and you are the establishment Mr Whitehall. I would imagine that Davis is the sort of person you would hate . . . fighting for the security of our country . . . rooting out the fat bastards who are corrupt and unpatriotic . . . and all because of greed and title. You are disgusting people! It is you who should be removed from office," shouted Ruby, angrily pointing her finger at the two-way mirror before Eric steered her very quickly and carefully out of the room.

Eric would have liked Ruby to have kicked him in the shin.

Eric's dad, Robbie was waiting in his taxi at the front of the building to take them home.

"All done you two? How did it go then?" he asked.

Ruby was quietly seething and it was Eric that replied.

"The interview turned into a witch hunt to get us to say that we had been working with their agent. I think they want to get rid of him for upsetting the establishment who seem to be more corrupt than patriotic."

Robbie was a quick thinker and came straight to the point.

"Is that right? So, did he recruit you, you and Ruby, to work for him? Why, you're only seventeen, the both of you!"

"It was our fault Mr Johnson. We wanted to be part of what we thought was an exciting game or adventure . . . and we pressured him to let us help him. All we did was make a few notes of when two of our guests came and went . . . that's the whole truth of what we ever did," gushed Ruby.

Robbie thought carefully. Was it not the same excitement and rebelliousness that made him join up with the Legion? Was he being two-faced on imposing a new kind of morality on Davis for allowing such a thing to escalate?

Eric looked at his dad.

"What are you looking at Eric? This is not a trivial matter."

"And your mates, the fishing trips each year . . . the re-living of the excitement from your own youth, dad?"

Robbie looked at him realising that Eric knew about his past military service.

"Aye lad, we all have the urge to live a life that seems more exciting and with an element of danger . . . but some of my friends were killed . . . as you were nearly killed."

"But we survived just as you did and we are better people for that experience Mr Johnson . . . just like my father, who showed me how to shoot a gun and pilot a boat. They are activities and risks all better off done and dusted. For one day such experiences could save the life of a loved one," argued Ruby quietly.

Robbie nodded in agreement.

"Aye lass, I'd like to meet your agent sometime to tell him off . . . but also to thank him for showing you both what really goes on in this world of ours, quietly fermenting away under our very noses."

Robbie smartened himself up and checked the rear vision mirror and side-mirrors before indicating and driving off slowly like a normal, typical cabbie.

"Not a word to your mothers about your spying . . . or my past, do you hear?" he added briskly.

"Thanks dad!"

"Yes, thank you Mr Johnson for your understanding," said Ruby.

Robbie looked at them through his rear vision mirror and smiled. His son had what it takes to become a success just so long as his girlfriend Ruby was around to keep him from living a life of mediocrity.

Robbie put his foot down and accelerated to over the speed limit before realising that he was trying to prove a point home.

He sighed and headed for home at a much-reduced speed.

Oh, the usual hugging and kissing and crying poured forth from their distressed mothers, now overwhelmed that their children who were thought to have been blown up were now safe, unharmed and perhaps a little more settled with life in Dogbol.

Life's Purpose

Time passes far too quickly, especially when we are busy.

It is the time waiting for someone or something to happen, the time spent with no purpose or belonging that grinds down even the most active person, if left to their own devices.

And so, it is with the idle rich, like generals waiting for the next ware . . . or like the empty meetings of the Cigar Club – gone to ground, waiting out the passage of time while their enemies and now distant friends find the time to forget and allow events to move on.

But what of the one and a half million dollars paid to Jeremy by the emotionless Chinese negotiator, Tan Ming Jie? It was not his personal money of course and one can imagine the feelings of those who chose him to represent their interests and values.

There was also the problem that the information they had obtained was worthless old site plans – and they had been flushed out into the open as the buyers of such information.

To lose face . . . and a lot of money is no incentive to merely move on. And then there's Tian and her diamonds assignment.

Would she forget that her mission was thwarted by two English children, playing at spying – falling in love with youth's innocence and chasing a sense of adventure?

I think that there is a cost in all this folly. For in the real world nothing is forgotten. The waging of wars, destruction of culture, social inequality and the abuse of innocent children continue on.

There is a cost and there is a deep sense of loss that can only be overcome once the fear and obstacles to moving on have been removed.

The Cigar Club was just such an obstacle.

Even within the depths of Whitehall there is a limit as to what members of the elite can get away with, escaping justice and being dealt with a light punishment if any at all.

It is to this end that operatives in MI5 and MI6 are trained to root out such obstacles to the greater good of Great Britain by being isolated from their shackles, at least within the cells in which they operate.

In the gentlemen's bar just off the foyer at the King's Club, a silent figure in a grey morning suit was reading the Times Newspaper, occasionally glancing towards the abandoned door of the Cigar Club meeting rooms.

Roger Davis looked a little tired but ever alert for the chance to gather new intelligence about the goings on at the King's Club.

He had now moved on with his objective of seeing the members of the Cigar Club brought to justice for selling secret government papers to foreign powers.

"Thank you Michael. I hope your wife gets better soon," he said quietly to the waiter bringing him another whisky.

The waiter nodded his head and removed the used glass from the table, whispering into Davis's left ear.

"They're meeting at two o'clock sir . . . Jeremy and Cartwright and Sir Rodney, Lord Roxburgh . . . oh, and Campignon is away in Whitehall."

Davis remained emotionless and continued reading the newspaper. It was now only eleven o'clock. He had made an appointment with a person from the Chinese embassy to meet him for lunch at the King's Club for twelve noon. A special menu had been arranged the day before by Davis, to suit the man's requirements.

After filling out the crossword and making a few phone calls to his superiors and field team, Davis watched as the shiny dark blue Bentley pulled up slowly in front of the club entrance.

It was exactly twelve noon.

The doorman opened the door to reveal a smartly dressed and emotionless Chinese man climbing out of the plush seating, warily scanning his surrounds. He had been there before with Tian to pick up the worthless documents from Sir Rodney.

Davis went out to meet him with a smile, offering his hand.

The handshake was typically soft but expected.

"Mister Tan, I am Roger Davis and I am very pleased to meet with you and have the honour of having lunch with you today."

Davis nodded slowly but modestly.

Mister Tan looked him in the eyes. Davis's intuition told him that this man was a deep thinker with a sense of honour and discipline.

"Thank you Mister Davis and may I say that I am pleased to meet with you also. I hope that a most honourable solution can be found to healing the rift and misunderstandings between our two countries," replied Mister Tan with a slow nod of respect.

Davis ushered Mister Tan into the private dining area of the club. Rich leather seats and thick pile carpet greeted the guests with an occasional aroma of fine cigars and delicious whiffs of 'haute cuisine' wafting from the other secluded alcoves as they passed by.

The maître d' showed them to their seats and presented a special menu written in Chinese just for Mister Tan, welcoming him in perfect Mandarin and nodding to Davis who appeared quite at home with the order of events.

A waiter arrived with a fancy glass jug of green tea and a carafe of Chinese rice wine.

Mister Tan was offered some wine by Davis and asked to choose what he liked from the menu.

"The Chinese chef here has worked in some of the best restaurants and hotels in Beijing and offers his greetings to you for visiting his exclusive dining room."

Mister Tan looked at Davis carefully, smiled and nodded.

"So, Mister Davis, you have done your homework well and know the values of respect, tradition and honour. It is rare to find such qualities in a man these days, especially in the West."

"It is rare that I can enjoy the company of someone who appreciates the values of his ancestral heritage. I'm afraid the West has always been a melting pot of conquerors and the conquered, with no lengthy dynasty of any standing except in recent history Mister Tan. Our latest religion worships the dollar I'm afraid."

They both gave a short laugh and soon turned to the business at hand with Mister Tan listening closely to the proposition being put to him.

Mister Tan enjoyed all of the selected food throughout the one-and-a-half-hour meal, including the Peking Duck. He was also entertained by having the Chinese chef visit his table to explain more about the preparation of the dish . . . in Mandarin.

As Mister Tan was leaving the dining room, Davis presented him with a small token of appreciation on his own behalf – a boxed set of two golden pens, one with the Chinese symbol for 'family' and the other with the symbol for 'honour'.

The usual interplay of non-acceptance of the small gift was eventually concluded with the humble acceptance and a nod.

Of course, this present would not be opened before they had parted ways. Culture and protocol secure many a friendship.

After Mister Tan was safely despatched to his waiting Bentley, Davis had just thirty minutes to get ready for the members of the Cigar Club to check in for their meeting.

He went back inside and settled into his usual spot overlooking the foyer and the Cigar Club entrance, raising the Times Newspaper up to conceal his face.

Sure enough, at ten minutes to two, a man in a dark suit stood alert, manning the entrance door, with his right hand positioned inside his jacket.

One at a time they arrived speaking briefly to the doorman. Davis couldn't hear what was said, but then he already knew the 'secret sentence' from previous surveillance. He went back to reading the paper, updating his photo collection every time a group member stopped at the door.

Sir Rodney was the last to arrive promptly at two o'clock as his black Bentley drove away to roam the streets, waiting for the exact moment to return.

"They say I may enjoy a cigar or two here?" asked Sir Rodney to the guard at the door.

The guard nodded and pressed the electronic unlocking device to open the steel door, still looking ahead at the front entrance foyer, as per usual.

Sir Rodney walked up to his reserved chair as everyone watched without speaking. He sat down, reached for his glass of whisky and after showing the glass to all around, turned to the portrait of Rupert Winston and delivered the 'entrance toast'.

"Here is to Rupert Winston and my fellow colleagues of the 'Cigar Club'. May we honour our values and value our honours."

"Bravo, welcome old chap," replied the others heartily.

Sir Rodney quickly gazed around the room. He was in an anxious state but resolved to show leadership with what he had planned.

He knew that everyone had been leaned on by the elite faction at Whitehall for having brought them into disrepute . . . and under scrutiny, by both MI5 and MI6, but more importantly by the unusual nature of doing business by a Roger Davis.

"All right chaps. You know that we have been outed for selling that worthless piece of garbage to the Chinese. In fact, that is what has saved us . . . the fact that it was garbage. We will have to do better in future next time and check the value of our merchandise," he said looking directly at Cartwright.

'Of course, I told the Prime Minister that we always knew it was a dud and that we were happy to make some money from the deal . . . and put a dent into the Chinese field operations.

Well, he was most impressed but a little confused because a certain little man had told Whitehall a far different story.

He told me that it appeared that we were selling secret documents for our own benefit. I put him straight on that one immediately. Our reputation here as patriots at home and with foreign governments as independent negotiators is a duality of purpose. Oh, Davis will have to go of course."

"Yes, quite so. Yes, he needs to go alright. I have been getting calls all day and night to retire from the House because of this. It just won't do," replied Jeremy.

Everyone agreed and nodded vigorously.

Jeremy raised his arm slowly and prepared to add some more to the issue.

"If I may, gentlemen. I have heard that the Chinese are not very happy about our little deal with those same papers. Naturally, we will have to pay them back somehow . . . but I feel it is not about the money, but more a loss of face it would seem.

And the matter about those idiot rogue CIA operatives losing our diamonds . . . to two children from the village of . . . Dog Bowl. Well, this will not do.

The diamonds are now part of the British Government seizure of booty from pirates . . . pirates they tell me . . . what with that silly fiasco out at sea where three parties were after two children . . . children . . . who incredibly commandeered the boat containing the diamonds, outwitting everyone!"

"They were British of course Jeremy, eh?" interrupted Sir Rodney.

"Bravo," shouted the others – all except Cartwright.

Jeremy continued his analysis to keep on track.

"That Tian was there; the CIA were there . . . and we were left looking like crooks yet again. We managed to talk our way out of this one as well of course . . . as no one was willing to testify as to what indeed we were all doing out there.

The Chinese and Americans claimed immunity. The Navy claimed the boats. They seized the diamonds of course . . . as you would."

They all looked as if they had lost all their fortunes at once.

"All the diamonds Jeremy?" asked Lord Roxburgh casually.

Jeremy looked towards Sir Rodney.

"Yes, well it would appear from talking with Cartwright here that maybe some of the diamonds are missing . . . about forty of them out of two hundred and forty-five to be exact, with a value of say . . . one million pounds at last appraisal."

The members' eyes grew wider and their interest grew stronger.

"Well, where are these missing diamonds then? Do we know? Does anyone know? I mean that would be a starter for paying back our Chinese friends, eh," asked Lord Roxburgh.

After they all settled down, Cartwright tapped on his glass with a pen to bring everyone to attention.

"If I may just make one remark about these . . . missing diamonds . . . then I may be able to shed some light on the mystery," gloated Cartwright.

He was always assuming a position of influence way above his standing within the group. After all, although he was a genius

I.T. man with rich and influential parents – there was not a title among them!

"Well, get on with it man. Where are they? Who's got them? How do we get them back?" shouted Sir Rodney impatiently.

All eyes were trained on the smug face of Cartwright.

"One of the children, the girl in fact, from the commandeered boat in which they had escaped from some Arab terrorists."

"They, Cartwright, you said they? Who are they? What are the names of these children and what do we know about them?" asked Jeremy.

Cartwright was hoping that his information was correct.

"Eric Johnson from the Mayfair Mews hotel and Ruby Peters, apparently his girlfriend . . . they went to the same school, are the two children involved in commandeering the rogue CIA boat with the diamonds. They did this purely by accident whilst escaping from the clutches of Scarab's ridiculous operation to abduct Ruby, in return for a ransom from the British Government. All happened on the same jetty . . . purely coincidental and equally dramatic events.

They not only escaped Scarab's boat, which got blown to smithereens by an unrelated official CIA operation, but then chose our boat, at random . . . with the diamonds."

There was a lot of chatter before Jeremy intervened.

"Mayfair Mews hotel . . . isn't that where Kasparov and Tian were staying Cartwright?"

"Yes it was. And it was also being watched by MI6 and more importantly by Roger Davis and his team."

Sir Rodney thought of all the implications arising from having every one of the players in their current problems centred around the Mayfair Mews hotel.

"Oh, err, go on Cartwright. You were telling us about the missing diamonds."

Cartwright was also thinking about the new information and how he could manipulate conditions to suit his retrieval of the diamonds and placate the infuriating Chinese . . . and get rid of Davis. He focussed back on the issue at hand.

"As I was saying, Ruby and Eric were on that boat. They escaped in a dinghy. The Royal Navy retrieved what they thought were all the diamonds having searched the boat thoroughly in Hull after it was towed in.

Now, Ruby had a black bag with her that supposedly contained her personal items . . . and well gentlemen, it looks like she may have pocketed one million dollars' worth of our diamonds."

"Can anyone see that we need to have her working for us?" joked Lord Roxburgh.

"We'd have to meet at her school," added Cartwright laughing.

Sir Rodney glared at Cartwright.

"And would you stake your life on it? This would be a most difficult and delicate problem . . . requiring the services of . . . a woman."

"Woman? What are you saying? We can't have a woman in the Cigar Club, in The King's Club . . . or working with us . . . it just can't be done, I'm sorry old boy," shouted Jeremy.

Sir Rodney remained calm and looked at Jeremy with a smile.

"So then, when are you going to be seen loitering around a schoolyard and interrogating this girl or indeed searching her and her belongings for the diamonds . . . if she actually has them?"

The others looked shocked. They had not thought about the consequences. This was surely the most challenging task that they had to face. Murder, espionage, spying, cheating and theft were in a different league to stalking and robbing . . . a schoolgirl.

What would the papers say? They would not be protected by their dwindling circle of influential friends. They would be finished. They would be imprisoned for whatever charges their enemies could make stick – true or false.

The remainder of the meeting was solely occupied with getting a suitable woman that they could trust to find out if Ruby had taken the diamonds.

Trusting a woman in this matter would be very important here. It was one million dollars . . . and diamonds are a girl's best friend.

Jeremy suddenly had a brainwave. A fact not unnoticed by the others because he always mouthed his thoughts nervously, without murmuring a sound, when he was thinking seriously.

"I say, I may have just the idea that could work. You know I've just remembered that our housecleaners' girl, Amanda goes to the same school, probably about the same age too. Well, we could get her, through her mother of course, to get her to find out who Ruby's friends and enemies are . . . sort of like a made-up background check for a fictitious job she could have applied for. And then when we find the girl who is her worst enemy, we can get her to do some spying for us . . . errr, through this girl Amanda of course."

It was a start. They all thought that it had at least some merit and all things being above board, they decided to put it into action. Sir Rodney then formulated their mischievous plan to get to Ruby and hopefully retrieve their diamonds.

The matter of Davis could wait for another day.

Ginger

A good two weeks had gone by since Eric and Ruby had been rescued by the Navy. They would be going to college soon and now was the time to relax after their ordeal.

Eric was busy working at the hotel making sure that Ruby was a major part of his time off. They went shopping together and spent time alone walking in the countryside and even fishing at the nearby stream which was partly dammed.

Ruby never mentioned the diamonds again to Eric as she had told him that they had been confiscated by the Whitehall man at their debriefing session. The day after returning home, Eric had bought her a bouquet of red roses and a bag of rock candy from the local sweet shop as a token of his love and understanding. It was a Thursday.

Eric thought that Ruby was unusually calm about handing them over to the authorities - especially as she had been so adamant about keeping them as compensation for her ordeal.

"I play not the 'vict-him' but I am the 'vict-her'," she had told him smugly.

The next morning, now Friday and the day that Eric works most of the day in the hotel, Ruby caught the bus into

Manchester - seeking out the apparatus for creating some safe havens for her diamonds.

She went alone, careful not to let anyone see her.

Jeweller's shops were definitely out as they would report her immediately. The sheer quantity was a giveaway . . . and they could be micro-etched with the supplier or owner that can be traced.

Similarly, using a bank safety deposit box would require her to use photo identification and her movements and deposit details could be traced, backed up by the expected bank surveillance cameras.

What she needed was an unusual place that she could access at any time without anyone knowing about it. Possibly more than one place, to spread the risk of them being found or her not being able to access them at a moment's notice.

Ruby considered the diamonds as compensation for all the stress and anxiety that she had to endure, nearly losing her life on multiple occasions.

She reasoned that someone had to pay.

As she got off the bus in the heart of Manchester with two large, thin, square packages, Ruby walked the short distance to the Railway Station and down to where the private lockers were located.

She returned to the station street entrance carrying one package.

Looking around, she continued down the street to the bus stop.

When the bus arrived, she was not there, but she had not caught the bus. Instead, she had hailed a taxi and was headed to the outer region of Manchester where she paid the driver in cash, then entered the 'Magic and Marvel' toy shop to make a purchase – ten Neodymium cylinder magnets – sized at half an inch diameter and half an inch in length.

She went out of the shop but then hurried back in to buy one hundred feet of nylon string and a box of ten ball bearings . . .

they looked just like the ones she used to play marbles with in the playground in primary school.

She looked around her again. Then, on seeing a fish and chip shop across the road, she indulged in a serving of two flake and chips which she had at the table.

On leaving the shop, she caught another taxi, this time to the bus station in the city. After again visiting a safety deposit locker area, she returned to catch a bus back to Doulton, near her home of Dogbol – only carrying her new purchases.

She entered her house, quickly looked around her, smiled, then waved and went in.

Davis was impressed. He couldn't have handled it better himself. He had four agents checking out the private lockers at the bus station and train station.

As the calls came in from the relevant agents it became obvious that she knew that she was being followed.

Mary was the first to call from the train station.

"My, my Roger, it's been a while since we've been made to look like fools. The package she was carrying has been torn up and thrown in the rubbish bin. It was just a blank white card with the words 'For Roger' and four kisses written on it. She never intended to deposit anything here mate."

Davis sighed and responded, "Thanks Mary. It's been a long waste of a day."

Then Barry from the bus station called.

"Before you say anything Barry, just let me know if there was a card for me," asked Davis angrily.

"Oh yes, there was a card alright . . . yep, certainly was and I quote, 'You keep yours and I'll keep mine' . . . oh and four kisses, with a PS, 'diamonds are forever, Scarlett'."

Davis was quick to brighten up. He even smiled.

"So, she does have them . . . I think I need to speak with her. She has already given the game away. A little careless I think."

"Good luck with that Roger. I fear she will make us look like fools if she keeps this up," replied Barry.

"Ah, we are already that my friend. I just don't want anyone else finding out or she could get hurt. We at least owe her that much . . . to keep her safe this time."

Davis started up his post office motorbike that was hidden just a short distance away from Ruby's house. He rode past her house. Ruby was looking through the window.

Back at Jeremy's estate nearby, Jeremy had made certain he was at home when the cleaning lady was due for her weekly session.

Jeremy's wife Belinda was always around at this time, worried that her house may be more likely to be burgled if only the cleaner was present, with the house being unlocked and the security system compromised. She had never really thought what she would do in such an event, other than call the police.

Belinda was mindfully disinterested in Jeremy's business, knowing that some matters are not worth bringing up.

Coming from a titled family sprinkled with rogues and a closet full of skeletons, she knew that some of his business dealings were not in the public interest or her own.

Jeremy had discussed his little problem with Belinda, albeit with a totally different set of circumstances, so that she only understood the main thrust of the request to the cleaning lady.

"But we already have a chef, cleaner, chauffer and a butler and a gardener Jeremy. Why in heavens do we want a young girl to be swanning around here with absolutely nothing to do? You're not going through one of those phases of old age senility where you have a hankering for the presence of young girls to make you feel young again are you? Well, it doesn't come from my side of the family." she joked, ending in a false laugh that seemed to go on forever."

She was feeling threatened by the shadow of youth and beauty intruding into her comfortable nest.

Jeremy was livid and upset that he was not respected in his own house, what with Belinda's family having a better pedigree and lineage than his own - a common theme in nearly everything she said to him.

Then of course was the money her parents had given to her which she had used to buy more than fifty per cent equity in their common estate to keep it afloat.

"That's not very funny Belinda. The girl is merely the focus of our attention because she has something of extreme value that belongs to me, taken from a foreign business partner.

For the very reasons you were thinking, it is most important that I am not involved at all. In fact, if you were more into taking an interest in my business and could see your way to do the job yourself, we wouldn't need Amanda."

Belinda had never bothered with Jeremy's business problems before, but was bored with her charity appearances and was intrigued that a young girl could cause so much trouble. She could also determine what was really going on between them.

"Tell me what she has stolen and I just might help you Jeremy. We never do anything much together anymore and I am bored stiff with playing the lady of the house with a lot of money."

Jeremy raised his eyebrows and looked over to his wife. He never really gave a thought as to what she did, being so busy with his club matters. He took a deep breath.

"One million dollars' worth of clear, white, large diamonds."

"A million?" shouted Belinda

"And, I some owe money to the Chinese Government . . . and they want it back."

Belinda watched as Jeremy lowered his head and closed his eyes.

"Most of my deals have been good, but this one came off the rails after we sold some goods to the Chinese Government that ended up being complete rubbish . . . and then when we wanted to convert the diamonds into cash . . . they were stolen by the British Government, with the girl in turn stealing from them."

Belinda was beside herself, knowing now that Jeremy's business reached within the bastion of Whitehall and thereon to the titled elite, of which her family was held in high regard.

"What have you done Jeremy?" she whispered, looking at him holding his head.

Jeremy sat up and composed himself ready for explaining his position to Belinda.

"There is nothing to worry about. We are shielded from any of this because it is my club that carries the risk. However, I am the financial controller . . . and anyway those diamonds are mine. They are ours Belinda."

Belinda thought about some of her friends and their children. Most were presentable for royalty and high society social events of any manner, but there were a few who had divorced, gone off the rails and were open for earning a favour or two.

"Ginger!" she murmured to herself.

"What love?"

"Ginger. Audrey's daughter. You know, the one with all those strange arty people at the mansion who act as if they are poor starving actors, with beards and scruffy clothes and everything – but who could probably buy out the entire BBC."

Jeremy looked at her sideways and straight-faced.

"What, she has a beard now?" he joked.

Belinda shook her head and smiled at him.

"I'll set up a meeting with Ginger. I think she must be nineteen or twenty now. Gorgeous long legs. We'll get her to suss things out and befriend that Ruby girl so that she can get the diamonds from her."

"Is she trustworthy . . . I mean with one million dollars worth of diamonds? . . . Long legs, I never noticed her long legs dear . . . or her other tangible assets."

They both laughed. Something they hadn't done in a long time.

"Right then. Set it up and we can be partners in crime . . . well, they are our diamonds, so I suppose partners in repossession," said a now more relaxed Jeremy.

"Done! I'll get onto it straight away. I'll go and see her now," replied his excited wife already heading for the door.

"And I'll send Wilkins around with the car."

Jeremy was very pleased with himself. He still wasn't sure whether Ruby had stolen the diamonds under the noses of the British Navy search party and then kept them after the Whitehall debriefing session – but he felt that Ruby was not the normal girl in the street.

After all she had defeated the CIA, the Chinese Tian and their own bungling Cartwright of the Cigar Club . . . and avoided being detained by the now deceased Scarab and his entourage.

He wondered how one girl could have amassed the skill-set to be so successful in surviving the world of spies and assassins.

"Yes Ruby . . . you have the diamonds alright," he whispered.

He picked up the phone.

"Sir Rodney . . . we are on track with the plan."

Friend or Foe

Ruby was down by the stream again, at her favourite place for idle thoughts, in a private space which she often shared only with Eric. It was a beautiful summer day amongst the lush country lanes and fields of hay bales . . . scenery and sounds that provide England with its unique display of true wealth.

Eric was still at the hotel, working wilfully with a renewed determination to pay his way whilst studying at college.

He was a changed person and he was madly in love.

The secret visits to the kitchen to grab a steak sandwich and ice-cold beer was a routine now accepted by his father for being a minor sacrifice for having his son return in one piece, from all the dramas over Ruby's kidnapping.

As Ruby was staring into the cool bubbling stream which was noisily making its way over the rounded stones and moss, she was surprised by a young woman silently standing behind her.

"Hello there, I'm sorry to interrupt your relaxing peace . . . but I'm lost I'm afraid. I came through the woods down at the bottom of that field over there and well . . . I just can't find my way back. I've been walking for ages," she said wearily.

Ruby looked at her soiled walking boots, green canvas jacket and light blue jeans before searching for her face hiding beneath a yellow wide brimmed hat.

"Oh, my name's Ginger by the way. I'm from London and I came here with some friends . . . yep, I lost them too," she offered briskly.

Ruby smiled at her and got up from sitting on the large flat rock.

"Hi, I'm Ruby. I live just down the road. You must have got caught up with all the fenced-off farms in the area. They can be quite difficult to navigate. You always seem to end up at the same spot because the woods obscure any landmarks," replied Ruby.

After more small talk, Ruby asked her if she wanted a drink . . . and there was one last tomato and egg sandwich left if she wanted it.

Ginger finished off Ruby's cool lemon drink from the thermos and scoffed down the sandwich as if she hadn't eaten all day.

"Look, why don't you come to my house. It's not far away . . . and you can rest up and have some tea. You can make a phone call for someone to pick you up," asked Ruby calmly.

Ginger agreed and off they went. The walk back took just fifteen minutes. As they walked, they talked about country life. Ruby mentioned that she was going to college in a week's time.

Ginger liked Ruby's house and was even offered a guided tour of the gardens surrounding it.

Ginger was looking at the layout of all the rooms and what they contained. Sure enough, one of the locked doors had a children's sign with the name 'Ruby' in bright red.

"I wonder who sleeps there?" said Ginger laughing.

"Yep, same door sign since I was about eight, I think," gushed an embarrassed Ruby.

After making the phone call to her friend Susan, giving her directions to pick her up, Ginger thanked Ruby for her hospitality and left the house, waiting just down the road near a big shady tree.

Ruby watched as the red Alpha Romeo stopped to pick up Ginger. The driver was of a similar age to Ginger and wore a beret and scarf over what looked like a black evening dress.

As the car accelerated down the road with a throaty roar, Ruby caught a glimpse of Eric walking towards her. He had waved back at the cheering happy girls which made Ruby quite smug. After all Eric was her boyfriend and not theirs.

Eric looked back at them and smiled to himself. He could see Ruby waiting at the gate and he forgot all about the two girls.

"Pretty, isn't she?" asked Ruby with crossed arms, pretending to be jealous.

Eric thought quickly as he knew Ruby was playing games again.

"Oh, I prefer British Racing Green myself . . . but then it is a hot Italian beast."

Ruby was about to punch him in the chest, until she remembered her vow not to ever do that again.

Eric put his hand over his chest and moved the now recovered shin to the back of his other leg.

Ruby laughed and did a quick Karate move which made him nearly fall over.

"I promised you to stop and I keep my promise, Eric. Anyway, it's not a good look. People seeing me beat you up!" she joked.

"For me or for you?" he replied with a laugh.

"So, who were they . . . those ugly girls in that horrible car?"

"Oh, the one in the yellow hat was lost. She was wandering around the woods and came across me at the stream. I just helped her out, that's all. Her friend came to pick her up."

Eric thought about it for a moment and decided everything was alright. I mean they were just two young women.

Unknown to Ruby for obvious reasons of maintaining health and a good relationship, Eric had placed one of his wildlife cameras outside near that old tree.

If anything ever happened to Ruby, he would be able to at least see who had been snooping around the house . . . day or night. It was fitted with infra-red LEDs for night pictures.

Eric was still worried about Ruby because of what she had been through, knowing that some people may not want to forget that during the skirmishes, people had died and diamonds were lost.

Further along the road, MI6 agent Mary Turner, a.k.a. 'Painter', had already taken photos of the two girls and recorded the Alpha's registration number.

"Coincidence and related criminal events do not make for good times," Davis had told her, convinced that Ruby was still in extreme danger.

Across the fields, a figure in black was retrieving a drone which had been quietly flying over the area for quite a few hours on observational sorties. The day's events would be analysed back at the Chinese embassy for evidence of unwanted intruders into their latest operation and for clues as to the whereabouts of the diamonds.

With the drone safely stowed away inside a backpack, the operator summoned for a pickup. A short time later, a small van with the signage 'Pet Shop Supplies' arrived to pick up Tian, the 'Taipan'.

Back at MI6, Davis was collating the day's observations from his field agents. Mary had been watching Ruby. Barrie Barnes, a.k.a. 'Owl', had been assigned to the ancestral home of Lord Jeremy St John Smythe.

Davis had been watching the Chinese embassy for any sign of Tian. He wanted to offer her a deal in which they would all be satisfied, leaving Ruby to live without any more fear of being hurt.

Tian had left the embassy grounds by climbing over the back wall, leaving Davis watching over shadows. He had nothing to report to the team meeting that night.

The meeting was conducted by secure, scrambled video link-up.

Mary had been checking up on the girls in the Alpha.

"The driver was a Susan Jane Fairweather, daughter of Lord and Lady Fairweather of Ashford Downs. The girl in the yellow hat was Chloe Helen Rust-Hallsworth or 'Ginger', estranged daughter of Lord Simon de Pennefort and an Audrey Carmichael. Audrey has a most interesting trail of misdemeanours that have been suppressed," said Mary.

"Rather upper-crust to be bothering our Ruby wouldn't you say?" said Davis to Mary.

"They were driving a red Alpha Romeo, registered to Horsham Car Rentals . . . and wait for it . . . hired by someone called Belinda whose credit card details says she is Lady Belinda St John Smythe," said Mary confidently.

"The wife of Jeremy St John Smythe! Good work Mary. That opens up possibilities for us to nail that Cigar Club rabble and take them off the streets," added Davis.

"Oh, I don't think they live on the streets boss. I've been monitoring his palatial grounds all day and I don't think he's short of a few bob," replied Barrie.

"The phone conversations of the girls and Jeremy's wife have been isolated and kept for future use by the courts," added Mary quickly.

"All right team. Good work today. Same again tomorrow, but I promise you that something will be happening very soon. I can feel it in my bones. Good night to you all," finished Davis.

Davis was worried about what might transpire.

He reached for his phone.

"Don't talk. Just listen carefully. I want to meet with you and Ruby tomorrow, Eric. Just tell me where and when and I'll be there. Probably better at a cafe or busy shop in the centre of town. I need to speak with you both urgently . . . but no cause for alarm. It's just tying up loose ends that I'm concerned with."

Davis waited for the meeting place to be confirmed.

"Roman 'X', where the sound of hens gather together to trade," came the cryptic response.

Davis sighed and raised his eyebrows. Had this boy not learnt anything about the seriousness of life?

"Right then, I have ten o'clock at . . . yes, yes I know the joke well . . . from my primary school days. Oh, and 'buk buk buk' to you too!" he replied with another sigh.

He arranged his schedule to meet them at the library.

Stone Fish

It was now Monday, with just five working days to go before Eric and Ruby started college. This calculation was not lost on Jeremy at Saturday's Cigar Club meeting.

"We need to get in there before Wednesday. Ginger said that her boyfriend and his cronies can break in there on Tuesday afternoon while Ruby is away at the bookshop with that boyfriend of hers and her mother goes shopping on that day. Thank goodness for routine and necessity."

They all mumbled and squirmed in their seats imagining what would happen if it went wrong. The full wrath of the law and the establishment would be on their backs . . . and the Chinese would still extract their vengeance to recover the money owing. The thought of any of them selling their properties to cover their costs was alarming. Sir Rodney was more forthright.

"Let's get it done so that we can contact the Chinese for a meeting."

With that, they completed the meeting rituals and left for their luxurious fox-holes out in the country, surrounded by trees, thick walls and the latest security.

At the library in Dogbol, Ruby was sitting at one of the large open tables in the centre of the reading room. Peering out of a large book titled 'Wonders of the Sea', Eric was scanning people in and around the library, as well as making funny unintelligible signs at Ruby.

Ruby looked once and then totally ignored him.

Davis somehow magically appeared standing right behind Eric.

"Playing shadow puppets Eric? What say we have a meeting, over there in that alcove."

Ruby laughed as Eric nearly fell over a magazine stand causing an avalanche of magazines and brochures to fall to the ground.

Eric quickly gathered them up and threw them onto a nearby table, quickly moving away from the scene of his embarrassment. Davis looked at Ruby and grinned. They settled themselves into the quiet alcove.

"You weren't followed, were you?" asked Eric nervously.

"We're here for a meeting Eric, not planning World War three . . . however I wanted to speak to you both regarding the closure of our . . . professional relationship. It should never have happened and I am truly sorry for the mess that followed. Now that just shows you how unpredictable things can happen in an instant," replied Davis softly.

Ruby looked at him and screwed up her nose.

"You want them back, don't you?" she said seriously.

Eric was stunned, but before he had time to say anything, probably out loud and probably in an embarrassing way, Davis briefly put his hand over Eric's mouth.

"Keep quiet Eric. We are here to finalise things . . . not to perform a theatrical performance . . . Now Ruby, listen to me. Those items are not your property. They are not mine. They do not belong to other thieves or to the government agencies of Great Britain. I need you to hand them over so that they can be given back to their rightful owners . . . in exchange for you and Eric never having to watch your backs in the future. It is widely known Ruby . . . that you kept forty of those diamonds and have hidden them somewhere. Am I right?"

"But they are compensation for . . .", started Ruby.

"Am I right?" demanded Davis.

"Forty diamonds . . . you kept forty diamonds!" interrupted Eric loudly.

"Keep quiet now Eric! You have just told everyone in earshot just what we are talking about. If you were mixing with the people that I am dealing with . . . you would probably be gardening now . . . from under the soil."

Eric realised just what a fool he had been . . . acting out his silly fantasies in the real world.

Ruby had begun to feel that she was way out of her depth and in real danger . . . as was Eric . . . or even her family.

"You can have them back. All of them. They are not worth the trouble. I'm sorry that I kept them. I thought the boat would sink and that everyone would think that all the diamonds had been lost," said Ruby quietly.

Davis looked at her obvious remorse as she almost pleaded with him and then with Eric for forgiveness.

"Thank you Ruby. Now there is one last thing I need to tell you. We have been looking out for both you and Eric and it has come to our attention that certain people have been casing your house," said Davis cautiously.

"What people? I haven't . . . seen," started Ruby.

"The two girls in the Alpha Mister Davis . . . I bet it was them," interrupted Eric.

"Yes Eric . . . the two laughing girls that you waved to the other day. The girl in the yellow hat, that you Ruby gave help and advice to . . . and then showed her around your house?"

"Bitch!" shouted Ruby, startling the elderly couple looking through the books on religion and culture.

"First off, you are safe. Second, I can assure you that we will covertly monitor you, your family, your house and the hotel twenty-four seven. We have high technology and a team of response personnel on standby. We expect something to happen before you visit the college bookshop. Just act normally and we will do the rest," continued Davis ending with a slightly curved smile.

"And third?" asked a stunned Eric.

"And third, I want those diamonds back now, from wherever you are hiding them . . . Ruby?"

Ruby smiled and appeared to be quite superior in the way she had fooled everybody as to where she had hidden the diamonds.

"Let's go fishing! I need to go home first and pick up my special fishing rod. Do you have any transport Mister Davis?"

"What do you want, a Bentley, Land Rover, Lamborghini, Van, Tractor or . . . a motorbike?"

Ruby looked at Eric and thought about the location.

"I think it's the Land Rover for our purpose . . . hmmm."

"Unless you have a Humvee with 'camo' markings," interrupted Eric.

"A Land Rover it is! Probably take fifteen minutes," ended Davis who pressed a button on his earpiece and enquired, "Got that Owl? . . . We want a Land Rover."

Sure enough, the Land Rover with a 'Veterinary Outreach' sign soon approached the library and parked in a no parking zone.

They all got in the vehicle and prepared for their mystery tour.

"So . . . why are you called 'Owl' then . . . asked Eric to the amused driver.

"Well, 'Diamond', it's a name I chose myself mate. Oh, and I see that 'Scarlett' is with us for an episode of 'Gone with the Wind' or wherever those diamonds have been deposited," said Barrie.

Eric looked at Ruby, closely.

"Where did you put them, Ruby? And when did you put them there without anyone seeing you do it?"

"You'll see Eric. It's all to do with the 'Magic and Marvel' toy shop in Manchester. I went there last week to pick up ball bearings, some magnets and a length of cord. Can you guess what I made?" teased Ruby.

Davis and Barrie weren't in the mood for games and Eric just shrugged his shoulders because he had no idea what he would do with such items. At least they all knew it was an outside location . . . well maybe.

Ruby went into the house and came out with a rod fitted with a ten-foot length of cord . . . and she was wearing waders. On the end of the cord was a solid flat plate about the size of a side-plate.

They travelled down the lane-way to a gate, leading to a track that made its way to the stream where Eric and Ruby often met.

Ruby waded out about one-third the way across the stream and proceeded to jiggle the flat plate, under the water, over an arc of about five feet.

As they all looked, she turned around briefly to watch their reactions as she hurled her catch into the air and onto the bank near where Davis was standing.

"Stone fish Mister Davis . . . forty of them."

"Well, I never!" shouted Barrie.

"Well done, Ruby. What an amazingly brilliant idea," added Eric, wide-eyed and proud.

Davis just looked and shook his head. He was thinking that Ruby would make a first-class field agent if she was coaxed and groomed to accept a position on her graduation. She was intelligent, cunning and showed no fear.

He looked down and examined the plate that had attracted a small bag underneath. He looked at it closely. An obviously strong magnet was sticking to the plate from inside the bag.

On opening the bag, he found eight sparkling white and wet diamonds, each the size of the large ball bearings that had been used to weigh them down.

Ruby was having fun as she proceeded to find the remaining four bags, each catch confirmed by a clatter of the plate as it landed back to the ground.

High above them, a drone was watching the entire operation, zooming in with its telephoto lens from a height of five hundred feet, merging in with the sky, its gentle hum drowned out by the sounds of the country and the stream.

In her hideout, Tian smiled at the goings on.

She reported back to her superior that his friend Mister Davis had kept his promise and so would be able to give him the diamonds in exchange for helping to bring the Cigar Club to justice.

Mister Tan was very happy. He was also very impressed with this most self-reliant youth. He had only ever come across this phenomenon once before.

"They call her 'Scarlett' and I am most impressed with her skills and ability to function in the most difficult situations of life and death," offered Tian.

"Like my own daughter in mind and spirit at the same age and just as stubborn and proud," came his emotionless reply - a most appropriate response from a man of few words.

"Now we must help Mister Davis with his own honourable quest Tian," he continued softly.

"Yes father, it will be done."

Deathly Peace

In a Kensington apartment on Balfour Street, number fourteen to be exact, Joe and Jay, the rogue American CIA agents who had lost their entire boat-load of diamonds to two English children were hanging out, keeping a low profile.

They were being sought for numerous crimes, the least of which was dealing outside of their jurisdiction in a foreign country, trading in diamonds and cash with criminal elements.

The real dilemma was that they had lost the diamonds that the CIA had obtained from a previous operation which were going to be traded for cash to fund other work in Europe. They were in big trouble and needed a lot of cash to disappear for a while.

They had also been doing their homework having tracked down where Ruby lived and had heard that she still possessed forty of their diamonds.

A simple plan was hatched to retrieve their goods and take another boat trip to the Mediterranean Sea. Their rental car was waiting outside for the trip to Dogbol, purchased under fictitious names of course.

It was six o'clock on Tuesday morning and the van was packed, ready to go. In Dogbol it was a cloudy day with the hint that it might rain.

By nine o'clock, Ruby and Eric were catching the bus to their college bookshop. With only a few days to go before starting college life, it was important to make sure that they had all the text books.

Eric had already been examining the on-line content and forming his group session friends ready for turning in his first assignment. He had no intention of reviving his ambition to be an intelligence agent or acting as if he was already.

Ruby was relieved that she had eventually done the right thing and handed over the diamonds to Davis. After all, she didn't want to have 'diamond thief' or 'defrauded British Government' etched into her official resume for her entire life.

That may have been a sticking point if she ever applied to the British Intelligence recruitment offices and had to answer questions about honesty, integrity and expectations about her career there. But then, they would already know more about her than she knew herself, including a psychological assessment.

Ruby's mum was on her way to the shops, unaware of all the fuss in the background. Ruby's father was away on business again in the docklands of Liverpool.

Her house was now empty. The road to her house was quiet.

At about ten o'clock the sound of motorbikes approaching from the direction of the Mayfair Mews hotel shook the quiet country side.

Both Milly and Robbie were disturbed from their daily work schedules, running to meet each other in the foyer.

"Another one of those damn biker club outings love! It would be fine if they came here for a meal as well instead of just passing through, but then the noise and their line of motorbikes would probably frighten some of our guests."

"Oh, we don't want them here Robbie. This is an up-market establishment. Oh no, we can't have that rabble affecting our four-star rating," replied an upset Milly.

They were about to go inside when Robbie noticed that the noise had almost stopped . . . down the road . . . almost down to . . . Ruby's house!

"Aye lass, you go inside and I'll just clean up my taxi for the airport job at two o'clock," said Robbie calmly, reaching for his phone.

Robbie could get no answer from Ruby's house and decided to investigate further, getting into his taxi and reaching under the steering column for his HK USP40 compact pistol. He had never had to use it in twenty years, but knew that it was never more likely to be used than in the weeks after Ruby's unexpected kidnapping.

He decided to ride his old bicycle, stopping a short distance away from Ruby's house, slightly out of breath . . . a combination of tiredness and anticipation.

"Come on, you old bugger," he whispered under his laboured breath.

As he lay down his bicycle in the grass, he noticed a faint figure hiding in the trees across the road from Ruby's, across from where four dirt bikes had been laid on the ground with the engines still ticking over.

He could hear what could only be described as the house being trashed. Glass was breaking and things were being ripped apart.

Robbie called the police and told them what was happening. There was no point him going in there as he would probably end up shooting someone. They were young, angry and they outnumbered him.

After a few minutes, they ran out holding various objects that they had stolen. The lone man rushed across the road and confronted them, asking if they had got the diamonds.

The youths were in panic mode and hit out at the man, knocking him to the ground. He reached out for his gun and shot one of them in the leg, threatening to kill them all if they didn't hand over the diamonds.

Robbie instinctively knew that he had to help and ran towards them with his gun pointing in the air. In a blind panic, the man shot Robbie in the shoulder which spun him around before he hit the dusty ground. He stayed down, eyes closing slowly and a feeling of impending death competed with a desire to sleep.

Suddenly two more men appeared from around the back of the house, also demanding the containers that the youths were clutching. They both had guns and spoke with American accents. Each second they looked meaner and unforgiving.

"Hands in the air, guns on the ground . . . kick it over to me . . . and keep quiet," shouted Jay.

There was a lot of suppressed whimpering and crying.

The youths put their hands in the air begging for freedom as the sound of police sirens could be heard approaching in the distance.

The lone man kicked Robbie's gun towards them which was picked up by Joe, the other American. His own gun had been thrown into the light grass the moment he had been surprised, just in case the two men had been the police or British Intelligence.

Joe motioned to the uninjured youths.

"You three can clear off now. I can't stand cry-babies. Run into the woods now before I start getting really upset and use you for target practice," screamed Joe.

The three youths immediately scattered into the trees leaving their injured mate screaming in pain, worried about whether he was going to live another day or die on a quiet country road.

The lone man remained with his hands in the air, remembering the location of his gun in the grass.

"And I don't know who you are mister . . . but we don't want to complicate things any more than they are. Keep your eyes to the ground and don't look until we are out of sight. Got it?" shouted Joe pointing his gun at the lone man.

Jay picked up the containers, put them in the rucksacks and used two of the motorbikes for their get-away.

After travelling only about a hundred feet down the road and around a sharp bend, they were confronted by Roger Davis and Barrie standing in fighting stance in the middle of the road, training their Glock .40 pistols at them.

The Americans skidded to a stop and let the bikes drop to the ground. One bike stalled immediately. The other still ticked over, labouring with its back wheel spinning.

"Move away from the bikes and get on the ground face first with your hands behind your backs. Now!" shouted Davis.

They dropped instantly and complied.

Barrie stood over them, securing them with handcuffs while Davis kept his gun trained on them. Davis put his foot on the motorbikes wheel which stopped the engine by stalling it.

"So, what do we have here then? What have you got in those packages? Who were you firing shots at? You can answer now or down at police headquarters," shouted Davis.

Joe realised that they were not the police. The police do not normally carry guns when doing surveillance on small country properties. He decided that they were British Intelligence.

"We'll comply with all the necessary protocol, but we are Americans with diplomatic immunity. We just happened on the shooting up the road . . . and . . . well we were looking to take the goods before those guys showed up. They belong to us anyway," said Joe hurriedly.

"Bugger me . . . CIA field agents," replied Barrie.

"Gees, don't we have any normal civilians in this country anymore? Everyone wants to be a field agent," sighed Davis.

Further up the road, the lone man could hear that the bikes had stopped. Knowing that the packages were in the rucksacks, he crept up quietly, dodging between trees and bushes to see what had happened.

From a distance he made out that two men were standing over two cuffed men sprawled out on the road. He recognised one of them immediately and prepared to take further action to satisfy his long-standing grudge against him.

Davis and Barrie had their backs to the man as he slowly approached from the tree-lined verge. Before Davis could react to his instincts, he was distracted by the American.

"Hey man, watch your back!" shouted Jay.

Suddenly four loud shots rang out as the man fired at Davis and Barrie in the back from a distance of fifteen feet. They were both pushed forward, crumpling to the ground without having any further thoughts, having had no time to respond.

"We honour our values and value our honour . . . Mister Davis," whispered the man to himself.

He then picked up both rucksacks and got onto one of the motorbikes searching for the electric start, unsure of where the gears were located. The bike burst into life. He kicked the gear lever to the floor and rode up to the two Americans. They were struggling to crawl away.

He checked the magazine of his gun. Smiling cruelly as they stared at him, he shot them both in the head with two precise shots before throwing the gun into the bushes as he accelerated away down the road.

The police were getting closer as the man sped down the road on the high revving motorbike. He could see the police car at the top of the road. He kicked the gears from first to second, revving the engine, spinning the back wheel on the gravel covered road, balancing his erratic driving with his right leg scraping the ground for support.

The police car screeched to a stop next to the injured youth and the body of a man. There was a lot of blood around the scene.

"Help me! There's a guy on my bike who shot me . . . he. . . he shot this man too who came to help . . . and there have been many shots down the road, just around that bend," screamed the injured youth.

"Holy shit! What's going on here? Get some back-up to stop that guy on the motorbike and have three . . . four ambulances here pronto for the injured," shouted the senior constable, "I'll check out this young bloke first with a hit to the leg. And the other guy has a nasty gunshot wound to the right shoulder. He's losing a fair bit of blood . . . so he'll need a compression bandage."

The senior constable reassured the youth that his injuries were minor and that he should stay still. Then he looked down the road to see if there were any signs of the gunman. He could still hear the motorbike travelling away from them.

"Go down and find out what has happened around the bend in the road, but be careful . . . wait, on second thoughts stay here and we'll wait for backup. He seems to be a shooter with lots of ammunition. We don't want to be next."

The motorbike noise stopped after the sound of a crash. Some birds flew up into the air about half a mile away, then everything was eerily quiet.

The senior constable decided to check out the scene around the bend after all. What he saw was a bloody massacre . . . with four motionless bodies splayed out on the ground.

Two had severe head wounds and it looked as though a staged assassination had taken place.

He examined them all quickly for signs of life. Three were deceased and the other was critically injured. He lowered his head for a moment before getting focussed again to see what he could do for the injured man, informing his junior over the radio that the man probably wouldn't make it. Then he noticed that the two men who had been shot in the head . . . they were wearing handcuffs!

With nothing more he could do, he ran back up the road to check on his junior partner Dave still waiting for backup and those ambulances. He could hear at least two ambulances and another car speeding towards them.

Junior Constable Dave Blackburn was partly in shock at the carnage and the sounds of the youth in severe pain made him anxious.

"I've never seen a dead person before Reggie," whispered Dave as Senior Constable Reggie Bartlett put his hand on Dave's shoulder.

"Are you ok lad? It's best to keep busy and concentrate on what information we can get from all this. Look Dave, you interview the young bloke and keep an eye on the other guy who has been hit in the shoulder. He's pretty much out of it but he should be ok. Check for any I.D. or paperwork, weapons or mobile phones. Anything they may have on them or around the scene."

"Right Senior."

"And I'll check for any identification on those four blokes down the road. Send some backup down to me and one ambulance when they arrive."

Reggie walked back down the road slowly to attend to the site of the four undisturbed bodies, checking the road and verge for clues as to what might have happened.

The Senior Constable got a huge surprise on finding the I.D. of the two deceased without handcuffs.

"Gees, these guys are snoops . . . MI6 . . . I'd better get on to head office. What the hell were they doing here?"

A long way down the same road, a lone figure in black was surveying the scene as best she could with powerful binoculars. It was Tian.

She had taken out the motorcyclist who had tried to run her over as he passed by, unwilling to stop as she had requested.

Tian had been watching the backs of the MI6 team, also expecting some form of attack on Ruby to get to the diamonds that had already been handed over to Mister Tan.

She was told to watch out for Davis's in particular, as he had been most honourable and useful . . . and he was so caring about Ruby and the position she was in.

Using her contacts with base, Tian was told that his name was Cartwright . . . but she had already identified him as the same man on the boat in the English Channel who had tried to kill her when they were chasing down the diamonds on Eric and Ruby's boat.

A little later she was told that he was the I.T. member of the Cigar Club . . . the one who had hacked the Ministry of Defence computers to obtain the garbage that the embassy had purchased.

Knowing that Davis was watching over Ruby's house, Tian could not understand why the police were the only ones walking about. Something had gone wrong. Davis was nowhere to be seen and yet would normally be in charge of the scene.

As the sound of more police cars and ambulances dominated her hearing, she decided to take the overgrown path through the woods to make good her escape.

Ambulances arrived to take Robbie, the youth and the critically injured Barrie to hospital escorted by police officers, while the bodies of Davis and the two CIA agents remained where they fell, waiting for the MI6 forensics team and the coroner to try and make sense of it all.

When his backup arrived, Senior Constable Reggie Bartlett carefully drove down the road, around the four discarded bodies on the road, heading to where the sound of the last gunshots had been heard. He met with another truly gruesome scene which shocked him even more.

Staying in his car, he called for an ambulance and for his superiors to meet up with him. He felt sick and overwhelmed.

One ambulance followed another police car down to where Reggie was waiting . . . where Cartwright had been killed.

Apart from the fatal bullet wounds to his torso, they had the grim task of retrieving his severed head that had rolled away from the totally destroyed motorbike, crumpled up in a tree.

About half an hour later, a helicopter landed in the field next to Ruby's house. It brought defence and intelligence personnel to investigate the incident involving their deceased operatives.

They were horrified after learning that one of their best field operatives, Davis had been killed instantly, with one of his team, Barrie having died on the way to the hospital.

The news that the two bodies in handcuffs next to Davis were CIA agents wanted by Interpol and of course their own people, prompted a quick call to let their people know their agents had died in a gun battle which also included their own agents.

They then directed the police about their business while conducting their own analysis of the situation. The containers in the rucksacks contained simple jewellery and a little cash.

At the Mayfair Mews hotel, Milly was searching for her husband Robbie, who had been outside when all the shooting started.

A police car pulled up to the hotel entrance. A senior officer and a police woman made their way to a waiting, anxious Milly.

"Are you Milly Johnson the owner of this hotel?"

"Yes, I am. What's going on, all that noise and banging down the road? And I can't find my husband Robbie. He went outside to clean the car and I can't find him." she replied fearing the worst.

"Let's go inside and I'll ask you a few questions," said the senior officer, "June here will fetch us some tea."

Milly started to cry.

"Is he alright, my Robbie? Is he alright? We have had too much trouble here and I can't take anymore."

"What was he wearing today, can you tell me that. I'm sure he will be fine but I need to know what he was wearing."

Milly looked up at the officer and wiped away her tears, regaining her strength to answer the questions. She had to know if he was ok.

"Well, he had his black trousers, his taxi trousers . . . a white shirt and probably a grey cardigan . . . it is cold today," she replied with a slow and hesitant voice.

The senior officer moved away from her and relayed the information to the central command for the incident.

"Right, right. Really? Well, how is it looking then? . . . right . . . right . . . well that's a relief. I'll let her know."

The senior officer returned to Milly's side just as a cup of tea was being handed to her by the policewoman.

"Now Milly . . . the good news is that your husband . . . Robbie is going to be fine. Absolutely no question about that, so you can relax and enjoy your tea. He was caught up in some trouble down the road and . . . he was shot in the shoulder. Apparently, he went to help some people in trouble and most likely saved their lives."

"Oh my! Why would anyone want to shoot my Robbie? It was those nasty motorcycle-people, wasn't it? Did you catch them? I hope they rot in hell for what they have done," wailed Milly before being overwhelmed by the feeling that Robbie was probably in a lot of pain.

"We'll take you to the hospital right now, after you finish your tea . . . and you can see him before his operation to remove the bullet and some bone fragments. Apparently, he is very lucky to be alive, but they are hoping that he will make a full and speedy recovery, so I'm told."

Milly was thinking at a million miles an hour.

"I've got to tell Eric, my son. He is away with Ruby at the college bookshop . . . oh Ruby, and Ruby's mum! Is she ok? . . . No wait, I think she will be shopping in the town. Oh, she has had such a lucky escape from all this. I don't want to stay here any longer. We have had too much trouble here and it was such a quiet village."

The policewoman helped her up from the chair.

"If you give me Eric's phone number, I'll break the news to him gently and get him to meet you at the hospital Milly."

"And Ruby too . . . don't forget to look after poor Ruby. She will be broken to hear the latest news about all this violence . . . so much violence in the world today," said Milly sadly.

As Milly was being driven to the hospital, the policewoman called a distraught Eric, with Ruby in the background screaming to ask if her mum was home and if she was alright.

Eventually, the gravity of the situation became very clear to Ruby. She feverishly dialled the number for Roger Davis. It rang for a while before going to message bank. She left a message for him to contact her.

Ten minutes later a call came through. It was Mary, Davis's team member. She sounded upset.

"Hello Ruby. This is Mary Turner. Roger Davis is not available for talking with you. How can I help you? Are you in trouble? I know about your Eric's father and I want you to tell him that I will meet him at the hospital. I hope to meet up with you too, to let you know about what happened . . . as much as I'm allowed to."

Ruby didn't know what to say at first.

"He said it would stop! He promised it would stop if I gave him the diamonds. Where is he? He lied to me . . . he lied!" she cried.

"Meet me at the hospital Ruby . . . I'll see you there."

Enough Reason

A hospital can be a scary place when a loved one is seriously ill or facing an emergency operation. Time slows down. The mind is occupied with possibilities and regret, for it is generally the time to meander through the important events of your private life, critically.

There's always the thought that you could have done more, paid less attention to the material side of life . . . concentrated on love ones and their troubles?

But we know that overthinking can be just wasted energy as time is a strange companion. The past has gone with no chance to change it . . . the future is merely a day-dream with which to plan and set elusive standards, if we choose to follow through . . . and then there is the present, the one instant in time in which we exist to do the things that make us who we are . . . in just that one moment in time.

Most often this happens at the cross-roads of life . . . the birth of a child, a marriage, the death of your parents or partner and the worst moment of all . . . the unexpected death of a child in a single moment of inattention or act of rage.

At the Doulton Hospital, Robbie was awake and wondering about his own life and family.

On the second level, walking along a narrow, light green corridor with dull lighting, two weary groups of people merged into the one waiting room with similar feelings until they recognised each other and found relief . . . back in the present.

Eric and Ruby had collected Ruby's mum on the way to the hospital from the shopping centre. There to meet them was Eric's mum, Milly and MI6 operative Mary Turner.

Eric ran to hug his mother and Ruby hugged her mother.

"How's dad? Is he ok? What's happening with the surgery?" said Eric, urgently.

"He's in surgery now Eric. They are removing a bullet from his shoulder . . . but he's going to be alright. He lost a lot of blood and there are some little bone fragments to remove but he's going to be ok."

Mary walked over to Eric and touched his arm.

"He lost a lot of blood but they are very confident that he will make a full recovery and be able to go home in about three days to rest up for a while. He was a very brave man, Eric. He went to help some boys that were being attacked by a crazed gunman."

Milly and Ruby's mum went up towards the nurses' desk to see if there was any more news, leaving Eric, Ruby and Mary together.

Ruby was seething. She paced up to Mary angrily and grabbed her arm.

"Where is Mister Davis? . . . He said that there would be no more trouble. He got what he wanted didn't he? Where is he? I want to see him. He should be here to explain himself after what's happened to Mister Johnson," shouted Ruby with tears flowing down her cheeks.

Mary also had tears in her eyes and turned away from her.

Eric realised that there was more to the story and Ruby was beginning to sense that there had been a terrible tragedy.

"Mary, what happened? Where is Mister Davis? Tell us what happened out there and why my dad was shot. You know he was ex-military, don't you? He would have known how to handle himself," said Eric quietly.

Milly was called by one of the interns. She went up beyond the nurses' desk to be escorted through to Robbie's bedside.

"You can go through now Milly. Only one person allowed at a time at this stage. He is fine. The surgery went well."

Ruby approached Mary and saw that she was trying to compose herself. She stared at Mary's tightly closed eyes and her deep breathing to calm herself down.

Eric looked at Ruby and put his arm around her, struggling to find the words that were waiting to come out.

Mary stood up straight and looked at them.

"He's dead, isn't he? Mister Davis I mean . . . he's . . ." started Ruby quietly.

Mary nodded and wiped her eyes. Ruby stared into the distance unable to speak.

After Mary had told the two about what had happened outside Ruby's house, her communicator sounded. She was needed elsewhere.

Ruby became very quiet and withdrawn, thinking intensely about how her decision to keep some of the diamonds had ended up costing lives . . . the life of Mister Davis, and the serious injury to Eric's father, Robbie.

She reasoned that it was all her fault. She had done that.

Eric could now see another side to Ruby. It was not the Ruby who was adventurous and playful, or the Ruby who had to fight off her inner insecurities at school or the terrorists or boat attackers.

No, this one was a sad, reflective Ruby who was now feeling great pain and regret, deep inside her conscience to where Eric was not welcome.

Eric put his arm around her, but she felt nothing but sadness.

"It's my fault Eric. I am responsible for all this. Mister Davis was a nice man. He looked after us and even guarded my house alone to protect me . . . and I let him down by taking those stupid diamonds," she whispered softly, "what have I become Eric?"

Eric gave her a close hug and stroked her hair.

"We are all to blame Ruby . . . with our silly spying games and making light of the work that he did. Stupid code names that mean nothing to anyone or anything but our egos . . . and the world we live in Ruby. The world we live in, that most people don't see at all. The world of Mister Davis and Barrie and Mary . . . all trying to protect our way of life and getting little thanks.

It's not a life for us Ruby. We must live a life that we can share as a family. My dad told me that recently. We must move on from this. Mister Davis gave his life for us to move on, together. He would have lived knowing that death was staring him in the face all the time. It was the precarious life he chose."

Ruby was listening to Eric's calming voice and the words coming from his heart . . . but she knew that she had to finish the work that Mister Davis had died for to exact . . . revenge and justice.

She had already made up her mind to extinguish the Cigar Club and its privileged members, protected by the elite . . . regardless of the cost to herself, for she knew that she could not move on with her life, or with Eric, until the deed was done.

"I want to go home Eric . . . alone. I want to tidy up the house before mum gets back . . . and to see the results of my stupidity," she said briskly, her mind made up.

"I'll be fine. They caught those thugs who broke into the house and I was told that a policeman is guarding my house until I get back because the place is unlocked," she added.

She would have none of Eric's protesting, but did agree to see him the day before college, for a quiet lunch in town. That was a start towards normality. As she walked down the long corridor and disappeared, Eric waited for Ruby's dad to visit Robbie so that he could have a talk with him about what to do.

But wait, who was that coming towards him.

"Kippo! How did you find out?" shouted Eric.

'Kippo' being the oldest and toughest of his dad's Legion friends was there to show support and to speak with Robbie on the quiet . . . to see what needed to be done.

"Eh, laddie. Ruby's father is on his way from Liverpool. He phoned me about an hour ago and some of the lads are coming down to see what we can do. Shooting your old man constitutes a call to arms Eric. Someone has to pay the price for this. How is he now? I heard that he has come out of surgery in good shape," he said roughly.

Eric had had enough of the violence and poor decision making from all parties, including himself.

"No Kippo! There will be no more talk of planning attacks on people we just don't know. We don't even know what really happened at Ruby's house or how my dad was shot. There is a lot we don't know and it has to stop. The authorities are working on it. Their top MI6 agent was killed! They must be able to handle it their way so that those responsible can be put away forever," shouted Eric.

Kippo nodded and promised that his team would leave it alone.

Eric filled him in with all the known details and each of them had a turn in seeing Robbie at his bedside, now able to talk quietly but freely.

He told his dad about Ruby blaming herself.

"You'll have to let her be, to sort that one out Eric, but keep an eye on her and tell her dad if you think she needs . . . professional help. You know, she has had a lot to deal with lately. I don't know how I would have coped myself. Probably would end up doing something stupid I suppose and getting into even more trouble."

It started to rain as Ruby made her way towards the hospital bus stop. A dark blue Bentley pulled up along-side her. She was not afraid, even though it was an unexpected event. She glared at the car as the window wound down slowly.

It was Tian.

"I think we have a job to do Miss Ruby . . . we owe Mister Davis a better send off . . . to finish his work. Please get in so that we can work something out together," she said with a caring smile.

Ruby nodded and got in the car.

"I will have some people clean up your home. You have suffered enough and your mother will want to be home with you tonight in a clean and tidy house," continued Tian.

Tian looked at Ruby who was still and quiet.

"Do not think about the past Ruby . . . that cannot change no matter how hard you wish. You have survived against all odds and now is not the time to wallow in self-pity. You are like me in many ways. You know, I too had such a time in my life.

It is only by moving forward with a plan that you can honour Mister Davis . . . to make your life, a life worthy of the values he believed in - justice and peace . . . by removing the bad people."

Ruby looked at Tian carefully. She seemed much older now.

"I will deal with this myself. I have my own plan which involves no one else. I must do it alone. Now if you can drop me off at the next corner please . . . oh, and I do thank you for cleaning my house. Perhaps we will meet again sometime . . . in happier times. I know Eric speaks very highly of you. You saved his life and you must therefore have saved mine. You do not seem to be like the contract killer that goes with your name, Taipan."

Tian looked at her seriously.

"It is always as a last defence, to take someone's life away Ruby. Always remember that they have family, a wife, husband, brother, sister, children . . . it is not taken lightly. What right do we have to take a life . . . if not in defence of our own life or that of a loved one?"

The car slowed down and pulled into a bus stop. Ruby got out and never looked back as she walked away.

Tian realised that she would have to be more careful looking after Ruby. It had not worked so well for Roger Davis.

She phoned her father who was waiting for any news.

"Treat her like your sister Tian. Mister Davis thought very highly of her. But try not to interfere with her mind. This girl is hurting badly. She needs to sort out her feelings . . . but do not allow her to make any foolish mistakes. She must renew herself . . . and not poison her soul."

Tian thanked her father and told the driver to move on.

Ruby was in the centre of town now, turning into Ardath Street to meet up with her father at 'Hazel's Cafe' as arranged. He wanted to talk with her first to see that she was alright and then to find out more about the shooting, before seeing Robbie and probably half of the ex-Legionnaires team who would be wound up for a fight and had probably had a few drinks.

It was an emotional meeting but they kept up their inner guard as always. After bonding with her dad in Scotland on one of his annual jaunts, they had become closer and she had become stronger. They had planned for any situations to arise after her kidnapping and as a last resort . . . there was a gun hidden inside one of the wall cavities of their home . . . strictly for self-defence.

"Look after your mum love and see that she is kept away from any dealings you have with the authorities. She worries about the slightest thing and may get her information back to front. Look, I'm going back to Liverpool tomorrow morning early and so I'll see you back at the house later on. You know if you want me to stay awhile . . ."

Ruby was most emphatic.

"No dad! Everything is fine now. The intruders have been caught and well you know the rest. It's all over. You go back to your work. I will be fine and will look after mum."

"Aye well, I know the authorities will be watching over you from somewhere . . . that's their job. We could even be bugged now . . . maybe in your bacon and egg sandwich."

They both laughed and talked about other things until it was time for Harry to go and see his best friend Robbie at the hospital, where his wife was also waiting with Milly.

Bad Habits

When Ruby arrived home, she found the road covered with yellow lines and the traces of black blood that had seeped into crevices and had not washed away with cleaning.

She could feel something in the air. She could see his face in the shadows and the blowing leaves. If only time could be reversed.

The house looked unscathed on the outside and was kept unlocked to allow the windows to be left open.

A policeman stood outside keeping guard.

"Hello Miss, I'll be off now that you have returned. You'll find that the cleaners have been very busy making things right again," said the young man with a smile.

"But they'll never be right again," thought Ruby.

"I hope you don't mind that I've been smoking outside. I made sure that the smoke didn't enter the house," he continued.

Ruby smiled at him but didn't reply.

"Well, goodbye then Miss and I hope that you can finally relax now that all this over. I was told that all the vandals have been arrested and that it was just an opportunistic burglary that went wrong."

Ruby wasn't listening. She had thought of a plan to destroy the Cigar Club forever. She could picture their demise, all of them together, falling like flies, tainted by the poisonous air, twitching and unable to breathe . . . or to make the faintest sound.

On entering the house, she found fresh flowers issuing some exotic perfumes in all the rooms and a bag of groceries on the kitchen table. The windows were open and a fresh breeze was wafting the curtains as if they were butterflies.

There was a note from Tian: 'Take the world lightly and your spirit will not be burdened."

Ruby screwed it up and threw it on the floor, then went over to open up her computer and logged on to the Internet.

She browsed for the information that she required and saved some photos and articles about a special topic . . . rare cigars.

About an hour later the doorbell rang. She looked cautiously through the living room window and was surprised to see a familiar man standing with a bouquet of flowers hiding behind his back.

She went to the door and looked at him fumbling with the flowers, offering her a nervous welcome as he thrust them into her hands.

"I wanted to see you Ruby after I hear that you have been burgled and Mister Davis has been . . . he has passed away. I cannot find out the details through normal channels and I know he was a big friend of yours. We knew each other well."

Ruby walked away from the door, so the man followed her to the lounge room. She placed the flowers on the table and slowly turned around to look at him.

"They shot Robbie too you know, Mr Johnson, Eric's dad . . . in the shoulder. He will be alright . . . but they shot him and killed Mr Davis . . . all because of some lousy diamonds Mr Kasparov."

Kasparov looked very concerned and was shocked.

"And Eric, is he ok? Was he also part of this shooting?"

"No, he was with me at the college bookshop and luckily my mum was shopping in town . . . and dad was in Liverpool on business. I could have lost my whole family Mr Kasparov . . . all over my greed to keep some diamonds that I thought . . ." she replied softly.

Kasparov was starting to understand the situation a little more but was still unsure of the events that ended with his friend Robbie being shot. Roger Davis, like himself had always been on borrowed time anyway, as they had many enemies who would see them dead. Even their own side would sacrifice a pawn for a king.

"Who shot Robbie, Ruby? Tell me who it was?"

Ruby's eyes lit up with anger.

"The Cigar Club . . . they are the ones who must pay for this," she said with determination.

Kasparov raised his eyebrows and nodded slowly. Of course, the Cigar Club had been under surveillance by Davis and his team as they had played off many factions to gain more treasures for themselves . . . even involving Ruby, Eric and Robbie.

"I believe your government will take care of these people Ruby, so that they never bother anybody again. I assure you. You may think that the likes of myself and Tian are just the same as Cigar Club . . . but we are not. We negotiate and spy and only sometimes kill, but only in order to obtain information on projects that may be used against us . . . or our people Ruby.

It is better to buy information from traitors and thieves . . . than for our countries to suffer many deaths from these evil weapons of war that are being developed. We only protect our country Ruby . . . just like Roger Davis."

Ruby had calmed down and understood what he was saying.

"Very well Mr Kasparov. I hear what you are saying but my government, Whitehall and the self-appointed elite . . . I do not accept that my government will rid this country of the Cigar Club, and I'm sure there are probably others just like them."

Ruby turned around to face the window.

"What do you know about rare cigars and their prices?" she asked slyly.

Kasparov was surprised. He wondered exactly what Ruby was getting at. Did she know about his methods of bribing people? He enquired further.

"Why do you ask this? I was not expecting such a question. Have you now taken up the smoking of cigars?"

Ruby screwed up her nose and smiled.

"I thought that I may deliver some rare cigars to each of the Cigar Club members . . . sent from a friend, to their meeting . . . that they may enjoy . . . oh for about twenty seconds, until the poison kicks in, Mister Kasparov."

Kasparov chuckled to himself and looked at her in disbelief.

"You have been watching too many old movies . . . 'The Three Stooges' perhaps or the 'Marx Brothers' with their funny exploding cigars my friend."

"But these won't be so funny Mister Kasparov . . . not for them anyhow," replied Ruby wryly.

They both laughed and Kasparov made himself at ease in a lounge chair.

"Tea Mister Kasparov?"

He nodded and thought about his supply of 'Gurkha His Majesties Reserve' cigars. Four or five of those would do the trick. It would be worth the seven hundred and fifty dollars that each one cost . . . but not to him of course. He knew the supplier.

After having his tea, Kasparov said his goodbye and promised Ruby that he would obtain some cigars for her loving gift-giving sentiments to the Cigar Club. He also knew the names and addresses of all the members and their habits . . . good and bad.

Looking back towards the house, Kasparov thought about how Ruby had changed from when he first met her in the restaurant of the hotel with her boyfriend. How could there be such a dramatic change, from innocence to becoming a willing perpetrator of mass murderer in what . . . four weeks or so?

He shook his head, yet understood the mechanisms at play for this to have happened. He would try and help her conquer these demons by getting to the Cigar Club first . . . but by more conventional forms of justice like stitching them up and allowing their house of cards to fall throughout Whitehall.

From a long distance away, Tian was watching the proceedings through her high-powered binoculars with interest and reported back to her interested father. It seemed that everyone wanted to help Ruby.

Tian decided to keep guard over her adopted 'sister', hoping to create the right moment where Ruby could overcome her feelings of guilt, whilst also bringing the Cigar Club to suffer - the style of justice that foreign agents have shared for many centuries.

Honour amongst spies was clearly evident in the world of Davis, Kasparov and Tian. No matter what the project or conflict of interests, there was always a level of professional respect for each other.

Cross Roads

The next day, as Ruby walked further into the town centre heading for the library, it started to rain again.

As she entered the library reading room she began to feel faint and grabbed hold of one of the bookshelves as thoughts of her last visit raced through her mind.

Eric had been playing at signalling with her as they waited and Roger Davis had just materialised from nowhere. She looked behind her quickly and smiled at her newly acquired cautious ways.

She sat down and waited, scanning the reading room door leading to the entrance and then all around her. He had not arrived and it was right on ten. She reached for her phone.

"You can't judge a book by its cover you know," whispered Kasparov behind her left ear, taking Ruby by surprise.

"How do you people do that? All that creeping around and instantly appearing is quite unnerving."

Then she noticed that he had a package for her and reached out for it. Kasparov held it back from her.

"Are you sure that this is what you want Ruby. These cigars are very expensive, very rare and now very lethal. I will take them back right now if you have any doubts . . . any at all," said Kasparov slowly.

Ruby looked at him and shook her head.

"Then, you can also have the names and addresses of the members of the group that you wish to destroy. A word of warning Ruby. Please do not go in person. Have a courier deliver them for you, from a cafe or business somewhere where you are not known . . . and change your hair, wear a hat or something else to make you look a bit different so that the courier will not know you," he continued, "and I also give you a USB stick to accompany the cigars. Sir Rodney is a keen fan of music. So please . . . one last chance to stop all this nonsense? Please Ruby, reconsider!"

Ruby took the goods and quickly turned away, thanking Kasparov and headed off with a determined sense of following her plan. She immediately headed for home.

Kasparov shook his head and sighed.

As he left the library, he found that the person behind him was pointing a sharp object in his back. Looking at the shop front window reflection, he could see that it was Tian holding an umbrella and she was not smiling. She looked annoyed.

He stopped and turned around, more welcoming than surprised.

"Ah Tian, how lovely to see you again and now you walk like I do in the sunshine with a lovely umbrella. Did they sell the Bentley? Are they cutting down on . . .?"

"What are you doing with Ruby? What did you give her? She is not in a fit state to be dealing with the likes of you and your people. I saw you visit her house," spat out Tian.

Kasparov pushed the umbrella spike to the floor gently.

"Come, let us have that meal that was so rudely interrupted by 'message bank' last time. We need to talk about Ruby. How about that Chinese Restaurant over there? Hmmm?"

"Huh, I never eat Western Chinese food! . . . So, what about the Hilton Hotel restaurant, your shout?" she offered smugly.

"Only if you let me drive in that shiny blue Bentley one day," he replied with a grin.

Tian held up her hand and to Kasparov's amazement, the dark blue Bentley appeared within a few seconds.

"Most impressive Tian! We go now and talk about Ruby. She needs some careful management . . . and I think we both need to get behind some guidance plan to save her from a lifetime of fighting shadows."

The driver opened the doors of the Bentley and they got in. As he sank into the luxurious leather seat, Kasparov vowed never to walk anywhere ever again.

The day before college, Ruby met Eric for lunch in town.

Eric thought that Ruby looked fully recovered when they met at the 'Princely Price Cafe'. When they hugged, she squeezed him tighter than ever before. She looked brighter . . . and felt warmer. When he opened his eyes, she was smiling at him.

"You appear to be in a good mood today, Ruby. What gives? Come on, there's something going on in that head of yours. What is it?" queried Eric.

Ruby acted as if nothing had happened in the last month or so and she brushed it off as if the outcome was merely a formality.

"Justice Eric . . . for what they have done to our country, to Mister Davis and to your dad. That's what is happening Eric. There is unfinished business that will not be dealt with by the elite . . . the untouchables in Whitehall and amongst the Lords of the land. It is our land too. Yours, mine . . . and . . ."

"What have you done Ruby? This all has to stop . . . right now! Have you not learnt yet not to interfere with the system? It may be corrupt and flawed but it is all we've got. You are becoming just like the others Ruby. You are operating outside of the law," pleaded Eric, holding her shoulders.

Ruby was not having any of this.

"If no one else will step in and deliver justice to those who have murdered Mister Davis and shot your dad . . . then it is up to me . . . regardless of the outcome. It is my life and I can do as I please," she shouted back.

"And who will deliver justice to you Ruby, for what you will have done? Where does it all end?"

Ruby glared at him and kicked him hard in the shin.

Eric slapped Ruby across the face which stunned them both. She looked back at him in anger and with a tear in her eye. She had crossed the line . . . and so had Eric.

"I'm sorry Ruby, I didn't mean to hit you. I've never . . ."

"Goodbye Eric . . . I never want to see you ever again!"

With that, Ruby stormed off, more determined than ever to meet justice out to the Cigar Club and this time with such anger that she had not felt before. The stress and anxiety from previous events were starting to catch up with her.

Eric was hurting too. He had struck his girlfriend across the face in frustration. He had lost her to the dark nature of the human psyche. Maybe he never really knew her at all. It could have all been just a crush that got out of hand.

Eric thought about life without Ruby – quickly deciding that his life wouldn't be worth living without her. He looked down at his bleeding shin. What would his father do?

As he looked up again, he was confronted by the close-up figure of Kasparov staring down at him, shaking his head.

"Don't worry my friend. You are both so much in love that broken leg and slapped head will be big joke in years to come. Next time you may have to shoot her in foot to keep her from getting into trouble, but you may need extensive surgery when she retaliates."

Kasparov laughed loudly and ruffled up Eric's hair.

"Come, we must talk. She is in great danger. Please sit down and we have coffee and English pork pie . . . I need this to think like a local."

Eric hobbled into his seat at the cafe whilst Kasparov placed an order for three pork pies. He was hungry for a solution too.

Kasparov told Eric about the expensive cigars that were laden with poison and that Ruby was intent on delivering them to the Cigar Club members.

Eric was devastated. What gave Ruby the right to kill? Why could she not see that justice must not be delivered in this way? Why did she not think about their relationship or listen to him?

"Do you remember Tian, the Chinese lady, Eric?"

"Yes, of course. She drove me down to the wharf area to rescue Ruby from the Arabs. She saved my life . . . twice!"

"Well, I have some good news for you. You see, Tian is working with me on this one. Like you we have the highest regard for Ruby and what she has been through. She is hurting badly . . . and blames herself for the death of Roger Davis," said Kasparov quietly.

"No. How can she think that? Oh! . . . those diamonds."

"Yes Eric, Ruby took the diamonds that everyone has been looking for. If that boat had sunk, as she had expected, then this would not have been a problem. But the British Navy towed that sinking boat back to Hull and found the rest of the diamonds . . . then realising that some were missing. Your corrupt people at the debriefing must have told their Cigar Club friends that there was an easy way to pay off the Chinese who were sold false information."

Eric stared out of the window.

"What are we going to do Mister Kasparov?"

Kasparov looked sadly at Eric and sighed.

"She will crack under the pressure Eric, I know this from experience and we must be there to save her from herself. It is not in her nature to kill people and she will find this out . . . but it may be at the wrong time when she is in very much danger."

Kasparov told Eric to stay at home whilst he and Tian monitored Ruby but that he should call her to try and make her change her plans. Eric agreed but other thoughts were running through his mind. If anyone could save Ruby, it was he. After all, he had done it before . . . with a little help from Tian.

After eating their meal they parted ways.

Across the road, an old woman with a walking stick was talking via her radio ear-piece.

"They've just left the cafe now and Eric's waiting at the bus stop. Do you want me to talk with him and let him know that we're looking out for Ruby and himself?"

"No Mary. Stay in the background. Kasparov and Tian seem to be offering some kind of help to them both. We need to make sure that they are not using these kids to do the dirty work of their foreign agencies under the guise of friendship," replied MI6 team leader Henry Roberts.

Roberts had replaced Roger Davis and MI6 had resumed the work that Davis was assigned to before his death which included working with Mary Turner.
As soon as Eric arrived home, he went to see his father.

After a brief discussion they both set off for Liverpool to talk with Ruby's father, Harry, about what they could do about Ruby.

Songs of Life

Ruby stared at the four sweet smelling cigars arranged in the presentation box with a letter. It was a personal letter from Kasparov. He had signed it as 'General Kasparov'. Ruby read the brief letter:

'Gentlemen, it would seem that I must remind you of my capacity to deliver not only financial offerings but also cultural gifts to please the senses.

Of course this is in exchange for forthcoming offerings from you.

Please enjoy this gift together and I look forward to doing business with you soon. I hope you like the music enough that it moves you to reconsider your lives – our lives. It is about the world we live in. The world we are making for our children.'

Yhere was also a USB stick, which was titled 'Games without Frontiers'. She hurriedly plugged it into her computer and looked up the file names. Some sounded familiar but she had not heard many of them before. She decided to write them down for later playing when it was all over. If Kasparov had chosen these songs, then they must mean something.

Placing the package into a pre-purchased plastic courier bag, she reached for her phone. She hesitated.

After a glance around the room, she removed the courier bag, took out the package and put it into her handbag, then went into her room to pick out something suitable to wear. Yes, that black dress with the zip on one side would be ideal. Smart enough and black enough to show her style and also good for fast defence movements, should she have any business to sort out.

After entering some information into her phone, she sighed, shaking her head slowly, until the phone rang soon after which surprised her. She let it ring five times before answering. It was Eric.

"Ruby, I'm sorry for hitting you. I was so angry about what you were planning and that you had kicked me again that I lashed out. I didn't want to hurt you."

Ruby thought for a while, staring out of the window.

"Ruby? . . . Ruby?"

"I'm sorry too Eric. But it's too late to stop me now. I have to do this or else I can never forgive myself for what happened to Mister Davis . . . and your father Eric . . . he was hurt and could have been killed. But I really do love you Eric, just so you know . . . if anything should go wrong," she answered sadly.

"But it wasn't your . . ."

Ruby had stopped talking, thinking . . . she was numb.

Eric shook his head, looked at his father and then at Ruby's father. The meaning was clear.

"Right then, let's be off to London," said Harry Peters, "my Ruby will not let up until she realises that she has made a big mistake . . . and that may be too late to save her. We're off to the King's Club."

A car pulled up outside Ruby's house. The driver got out to open the door for his expected passenger. The Uber taxi had arrived to take her to the bus station in Doulton.

The driver found Ruby to be very quiet and understood that she didn't want to be disturbed. He was courteous and friendly with a warm smile for her when she got out at the station.

He wondered about this girl in the smart black dress and black hat, imagining that she may be going to a funeral.

Ruby made her way to the ticket office.

"Single ticket to South Kensington Station please."

"Yes love, here you are. Going to the big smoke, are you?" asked the pleasant railway attendant.

Ruby thought how silly her answer would appear if the attendant knew what she was going to do.

"Big smoke? Yes . . . big smoke, that's what I'm doing," she replied with a gentle smile.

The attendant looked at her clothes as she walked slowly towards the platform.

"Poor lass, she must have lost a loved one," he whispered to the next in line at the counter.

Ruby entered the carriage which was half full and pulled out her I-phone to listen to some music. She dialled in 'Games without Frontiers' and turned up the volume. She had never heard the music before and became immersed in its message.

She looked at Kasparov's music list. There was 'The Carpet Crawlers' followed by Sting with 'Russians'.

"Mister Kasparov. You have a sense of the moment for even the most solemn of duties. These people will pay their price, if not today then tomorrow," she whispered to herself.

She looked at the music list again. The final two tracks was Billy Joel singing 'Leningrad' and then 'Yesterday When I Was Young' sung by Charles Aznavour.

It looked sad. She dialled up some more familiar music to pass the time and then just stared out of the window immersed in her daydreams with images of the Cigar Club falling like flies around their meeting room table.

It wasn't long before the train reached South Kensington Station. It was quite busy. Anything was busy compared to Dogbol or even Doulton for that matter.

Ruby had learnt from her intelligence agency debriefing session at Hull that the Cigar Club was based in rooms within The King's Club, an exclusive men's club in Kensington.

As she wouldn't be allowed in, the cigars would have to be delivered by hand to the doorman. That was safe enough.

A taxi was summoned at the station entrance and Ruby explained that she wanted to go to The King's Club to deliver a package to the doorman.

"Blimey Miss, that's an upper crust pub if ever I saw one. They usually get limousines and government agencies to drop people off there. They say that's where spies and crooks get together . . . oh and those politicians, but then we can put them down as being in the same category in many cases," said the driver looking her up and down quickly.

Ruby smiled and nodded.

"Make sure you wait for me won't you, I don't want to have to come looking for you?"

"No Miss, you may set those faceless scoundrels onto me otherwise," he joked.

Ruby selected some of the music tracks from Kasparov's list as the taxi made its way through the busy streets.

"How people suffer so," she whispered quietly, her eyes tearing up, her throat hard . . . her mind suspended in isolated intense thoughts – flashes of her short life which had already been filled with such intense moments - moments that a girl should not experience in modern day England during peace time.

Tears unable to be suppressed, flowed freely as her mind drifted wildly between images of Eric helped by Tian, the praise that Robbie had lavished on Kasparov and the seldom smiling, ever alert Davis who had met his end doing his job.

She thought more about her times with Eric.

"Dear Eric," she murmured, shaking, thinking of Eric, the school nerd who had become a man, travelling the darkest of paths just to be with her.

He had saved her life . . . and yet she had turned his life upside down. It was she who had caused the death of Mister Davis and the shooting of Eric's father, Robbie. What had they done to deserve this?

The driver looked at Ruby occasionally and wondered if he should say anything. He decided that the girl needed some space before confronting what may be a funeral or sad event.

The front of the hotel was blocked by a black Bentley with its door open and the chauffeur waiting, looking bored with his eyes closed. The taxi had to park about forty feet away as the doorman would get most disturbed at having a common taxi at his doors.

Ruby got out of the taxi and walked towards the entrance.

The chauffeur now opening his eyes to see whether his boss had arrived caught a glimpse of this smart, attractive girl in the black evening dress . . . then he looked at her sad face hiding under that flat black hat.

"It's the girl. Yes, it's her alright," whispered the chauffeur to the passenger in the back seat.

"Who? What girl are you talking about Wilkins?"

"It's that Ruby girl that caused us all that bother, Sir Rodney. The one that had the diamonds and all."

Sir Rodney looked at her approaching the car. He looked all around him. The doorman was busy, the street was quiet and the door of his car was open.

As she passed by, Ruby was having second thoughts about carrying out her mission. She stopped, hesitated and turned around to go back to the waiting taxi.

Sir Rodney instinctively made his move, grabbed her arm and pushed her into the car ahead of him. He covered her mouth and shouted at Wilkins.

"Get in and drive off now. Quickly! And don't stop! I want to have a word with the famous, invincible Ruby."

The Bentley sped off down the street now with Sir Rodney holding a knife to Ruby's neck to keep her quiet. He activated his phone to call Jeremy.

"Jeremy we've taken your car for a run around the block. We've picked up a very interesting person for you to talk to. Ruby Peters. Yes, the girl on the boat . . . who stole our diamonds!"

The abduction did not go unnoticed.

Tian and Kasparov had been following her all the way from Dogbol and were scrambling to get their vehicle to come back for them after being dropped off. They had been totally caught out by this surprise move.

Further down the road, Eric, Robbie and Harry were watching the whole thing, having followed her taxi from the train station, again expecting that Ruby would only deliver the cigars and head back home.

"She's gone! They've taken her. Quick get on their tail and ram the bastards if necessary. We're not losing her again," shouted Ruby's father, Harry.

Eric and Robbie were tense and the adrenalin was pumping.

Robbie put his foot down . . . and then came to a screeching halt.

"Get in you two. Get in!" he shouted to Tian and Kasparov.

Robbie again put his foot down and sped off after the Bentley.

Tian and Kasparov checked their revolvers and Eric and Harry scoured the road ahead for signs of the Bentley.

Jeremy was coming out of The King's Club still holding his phone. It was obvious that the doorman had seen at least part of what was going on.

Jeremy looked at him, shook his head quickly and then saw the empty taxi waiting up ahead.

"I'll see you right Max. Just a bit of a domestic problem, that's all," he whispered as he passed the doorman.

Jeremy got in the back of the taxi before the driver knew what was going on.

"Here mate, this taxi is booked. You can't get in here!"

Jeremy reached into his jacket and pushed the snub end of his Makarov pistol – another present from Kasparov, into the driver's neck, smiling and making sure that he avoided giving anything away to the security camera mounted above the driver.

"Drive and you won't get hurt. Take me a few blocks away quickly . . . and don't activate any alarms."

The taxi driver followed his instructions and was relieved to be rid of the man. He accelerated away and thought twice about calling the police. Who was he anyway in the scheme of things?

"Blimey all that for nothing. Lost me fare and that old bastard just got a free ride," he murmured before immediately swinging around to go back to the King's Club.

The girl in the black dress was not there and the doorman just shrugged his shoulders.

Meanwhile as Jeremy was trying to phone for his own car to pick him up, another Bentley pulled up beside him. It was a dark blue colour.

"That was quick . . . I never . . ."

The window wound down and as if in slow motion an elderly Chinese man looked out at him with no expression.

Two quick shots sounded like puffs of air and Jeremy fell to the floor. He had met with Mister Tan, the negotiator.

The Cigar Club account had now been closed.

The car slowly drove off as the window wound up.

Robbie was caught up in traffic and Jeremy's black shiny Bentley, now carrying Sir Rodney and Ruby was nowhere to be seen.

They were anxious and annoyed that Ruby had disappeared again. They argued amongst themselves as to where she would be taken. They didn't have to think for long. Eric's phone was being called. He looked at the caller ID. It said Roger Davis, but how can that be!

"Eric, Eric I know where you are and who you are with. I know Ruby has been abducted and we are after that car at this very moment. They seem to be going to Sir Rodney's estate. I want you all to keep away and let us do our work. Too many people involved will make Sir Rodney very unpredictable . . . and he may take his revenge out on Ruby or try to eliminate any evidence. Got it!" shouted MI6 team leader Henry Roberts.

"Got it Mister Roberts," said Eric before getting cut off.

Eric told the others and it was instantly and unanimously agreed that no government department was going to be responsible for saving Ruby ever again.

"I know where it is. We have plans of entire estate from previous surveillance," rushed Kasparov.

"So do we Ilya. I suggest we get into position as quickly as possible," said Tian with authority.

"Keep her safe at all times," added Harry.

"Aye, they'll do a far better job than the likes of us two Harry, or that mob down at MI6 or MI5 or whatever they call themselves these days," said an anxious Robbie.

Eric feared for the worst and knew that he must play his part even if meant that he would lose his life trying to save her. How much luck can a man have?

"She still thinks those cigars are poisoned too. I hope she's not relying on that fact to get her through," murmured Eric to Tian.

Tian was fuming.

"Well, that life lesson turned out for the best didn't it," she said poking Kasparov in the ribs.

"But at least she hesitated and was about to walk back to the taxi. She knew that she couldn't go through with it. She's no killer is my Ruby," replied Eric proudly.

"She's the best Eric; she's my brave and beautiful girl . . . just had too much happen to her in such a short time. I hope I trained her well," added Harry looking a little brighter.

Eric looked at his recovering shin and knew who to blame.

Harry was watching, wincing as he felt Eric's shin pain.

"Aye lad, the shin is always the first step . . . before much more lethal and eye-watering solutions are introduced."

"She's won awards son, lots of them . . . and all on account of being bullied in primary school," added Robbie with a wink.

Carpe Diem

Ruby stared at the four walls of the private meeting room in Sir Rodney's grand house on his estate.

Perimeter security was very tight with armed guards patrolling the grounds. One of them was standing right next to Ruby, holding the back of her neck firmly.

The presentation case of cigars was in front of her but her handbag had been confiscated and was being searched.

Lord Roxburgh and Roland Campignon had been called to attend a rushed meeting during the drive to the estate. Jeremy was not answering his phone. Sir Rodney thought the worst.

With Cartwright having met a most fitting end in a deadly gun fight according to Sir Rodney for trying to steal the diamonds for himself, the ranks were thinning. Cartwright was a traitor to the Cigar Club code of conduct. Well, even an elite group of bandits can have some sense of hypocrisy.

Sir Rodney entered the room quickly, sat down and looked across at Ruby. He raised his eyebrows and looked quite smug.

"Ruby Peters. All dressed up with nowhere to go . . . and what do you have for me there in that little box? It looks like a presentation box of 'Gurkha His Majesties Reserve' . . . made with special eighteen-year-old cigars soaked in an entire bottle of 'Louis XIII de Rémy Martin' cognac. Doesn't it just roll off the tongue with extravagance? Seems such a waste of cognac . . . but oh what a beautiful cigar it makes. All gone up in a few puffs of smoke too except for the memories remaining," he gloated.

Ruby looked at him sternly, imagining him falling off his chair, writhing around in absolute pain.

"And a letter too, how nice. From General Kasparov no less . . . and why would you have a present to deliver to me from a Russian agent? Unless you stole it of course. I mean that would be typical of your modus operandi. Stealing diamonds, stealing boats and now stealing expensive cigars. Yes, it all fits."

His analysis was interrupted by the arrival of Lord Roxburgh and Roland Campignon. Each stared at the elusive master thief and escape artist sitting before them. Roxburgh touched her hair and held up her chin so that he might look at her directly.

Ruby looked away. She was analysing an escape route and working out who to attack first should the occasion arise.

"Look gentlemen, the bearer of gifts from this beautifully dressed young woman, with a letter from dear Ilya and what's this? . . . a USB stick with some music? See how carefully the cigars have been arranged . . . just the four and so much thought put in to mesmerise us into thinking we must trust her. She was about to run away when I caught her with this box."

"Where's Jeremy?" asked Campignon.

"Where indeed. I'm afraid that our 'Trojan Horse' here could be the bearer of bad tidings and that we may never see our Jeremy again. I think we must check our security system quickly and plan for a trip to . . . well I can't say . . . unless our guest here meets an unfortunate accident like tripping over her pretty dress in front of the vicious, hungry guard dogs," replied Sir Rodney now with a mean look and changed attitude.

The sound of a helicopter passing high overhead had them all running towards the window.

The MI6 team were regrouping on the river side of the estate whilst Robbie, Harry, Eric, Tian and Kasparov were preparing for immediate assault from the main entrance. It would be least expected attack route and so have the most likely chance of not being noticed.

Ruby looked at them gathered around the window, hiding behind the curtains. She smiled lightly and tried to get up. The guard held her down. How she would love to give him a few kicks to remember her by.

"We are all going to die today . . . you, me, your silly club and what you stand for. You are traitors to your country and should be destroyed," said Ruby with an air of authority.

Sir Rodney laughed out loud.

"See, now she can talk. Now I don't know about you Ruby, but we have an escape route to paradise . . . whilst you have a box of cigars, a flowery letter and some emotional music to die by. I wonder if the 1812 overture is on there too."

"You may as well smoke your cigars and have a stiff drink. It may be your last," she replied, looking at the cigars.

Sir Rodney watched her closely. Had she messed up?

Just then the perimeter alarm sounded from next to the main entrance. Eric had run ahead of Tian and Kasparov and had scaled the wall, working his way towards the east wing of the estate. His absence was not noted for five minutes.

"Where's Eric? Where's he gone?" shouted Robbie.

Robbie ran to climb the perimeter wall but was hauled down by Harry and Kasparov.

"Stay here both of you! I will go with Tian to rescue them. Do not move from here, we will need you here," shouted Kasparov firmly.

With that Kasparov and Tian quickly scaled the wall, dropped down between some trees and went either side of the main pathway using the line of bushes and statues as cover.

Eric had now reached a side window of the house and used his home-made glass cutter with vibrator attached to create a hole big enough to put his hand through to open it.

He dropped inside the room and was about to make for the door when a security guard came up from behind and grabbed him. The guard also had a gun.

Eric was dragged into to the same room as where Ruby was being held and was thrown to the ground.

"Eric! No Eric! What are you doing here? You shouldn't have come," cried Ruby.

"Ruby. Are you alright? Have they hurt you at all? If they have, I'll kill them all myself," replied Eric angrily.

Sir Rodney laughed. Then he thought about what Eric had said and looked at the cigars again . . . then back at Ruby who had beads of perspiration on her forehead . . . then finally at a regretful Eric. He had made a grave mistake.

"Ah, yes Kasparov and his little present for his English friends. Well, it would be a shame to waste these on ourselves gentlemen and have our guests miss out on such a fine luxury . . . so I invite you Eric . . . to sample one of these seven-hundred-and-fifty-dollar cigars to show your girlfriend here that you are indeed a man of fine taste and precise words of wisdom."

"We don't smoke your toffee-nosed rubbish . . . not anything, so you'd be wasting them when you obviously like them and went to great trouble to get them," chimed in Ruby nervously.

It dawned on Eric that Ruby still didn't know that the cigars were in fact not poisoned and that there was a way out if only he could get to talk with her.

"I want to have a quiet moment with Ruby before you make us smoke those cigars . . . at least give me that," asked Eric.

Ruby was shaking and the guard was allowed to let her up to see Eric. He held her tight as she was trying to say a million things to him . . . but finally he got to whisper to her.

"There is no poison. Play dead after you smoke for about twenty seconds. I love you."

Ruby and Eric had a final look at each other. They now had an understanding that they both had to put on an act like never seen before.

"Ah, how sweet. They are going to play Romeo and Juliet together. Such sweet revenge for the intruding parties to find them as we disappear," teased Sir Rodney.

He pushed the cigars over to them and got out his gold lighter from his top pocket. He was oblivious to the sounds of more security alarms indicating further breaches to the house.

"Now, smoke these while I watch you wither. Roland, Roxburgh, get down to the helicopter pad under the house. I'll be there soon. This shouldn't take too long if I remember."

Roxburgh, Roland and the guard rushed out of the room. Sir Rodney lit up the two cigars while holding a gun at them.

"I'm sorry but it's either the cigars or the gun. Oh, what a typical Russian solution from dear Kasparov. Why I know he has used the same technique before."

Eric and Ruby started puffing on the cigars.

"Inhale you two! No blowing kisses to each other," shouted Sir Rodney laughing at the extreme hurt he would do to the families of these two nuisances.

Suddenly, Eric started to roll his eyes and grab his chest, making all sorts of grunting and groaning noises. Ruby kept staring at Sir Rodney.

Eric fell to the floor in front of Sir Rodney, rolling and writhing, then pulling at his trousers, shoes, with much moaning and groaning.

As Sir Rodney looked down at him, Ruby let fly with a swirling kick to his head. The gun fired into the air as he fell to the floor, dropping the gun, allowing Eric to grab it.

Ruby followed through with a karate punch to the throat, a kick to the groin, a sweeping kick to the legs and finally a stomp onto his throat as he lay gasping for air on the ground.

"If he moves, shoot him 'Diamond' just like you did with all the others."

Eric was frozen with excitement and yet amazed at just what Ruby had done . . . all on her own. His own shin injury was merely a bruise compared to that impressive walloping.

"I jest at wounds that never left a scar," he started, much to Ruby's amazement.

She took the gun off Eric and pointed it at Sir Rodney's face.

At that same moment in time Kasparov and Tian burst into the room with guns drawn, rolling over as they surveyed the occupants for injury and for any further signs of danger.

They looked at each other, smiled and jumped to their feet, checking to see if any of them needed help. Kasparov kept a gun trained on Sir Rodney. Tian took the gun from Ruby and put her arm on Ruby's shoulder.

Ruby went over to her hero, Eric.

"Great acting Diamond . . . so you did know that the safety catch was on right?" said Ruby quietly before giving him a big hug and a kiss.

Eric looked at her calmly, nodding his head.

"Just one of my moves Scarlett. I had him licked the moment I grabbed his gun. You know . . . it was the intention and not the actual act of shooting that was my strength," replied Eric matter-of-factly.

"One of your moves? You have moves now? Why you pompous ham! . . . but again you saved my life Eric . . . please never stop doing that!"

They hugged each other again and Ruby planted a real smacker on his lips. No, it was a kiss . . . she didn't hit him.

Ruby caught a glimpse of Tian looking at Kasparov. A look that was returned. A look that she was now most familiar with.

"The other two are down below in a helicopter bay," rushed Eric, suddenly remembering Sir Rodney's plan.

Tian nodded and watched Kasparov eyeing up the smouldering expensive cigars. He casually picked one up and put it to his mouth. Tian had no time to relax now. She had loose ends to tie up.

"You and your life lessons Ilya! Stay here and I'll get the other two," she said briskly, watching Kasparov taking another puff on the cigar, not intending to go anywhere.

"I couldn't go through with it . . . I have no right to kill anyone Mr Kasparov," said Ruby quietly.

"Well, I knew you would come to see reason Ruby. You were just really upset and lashed out . . . just like I was. We've been through a lot, you and me. We must have nine lives like a cat," said Eric thoughtfully.

The sound of shooting coming from below the house was brief but intense before everything went quiet. Tian had met up with the MI6 team coming from the helicopter bay with three prisoners. They had given up without much of a fight.

"I told you to keep away Tian. You and your band of super heroes," boomed Henry Roberts.

Tian looked at him, pointing her finger angrily.

"You would have been too late to save the girl. If it hadn't been for Eric's quick thinking they would both be dead . . . another two bodies to cope with . . . and mere children too. This is the end of the Cigar Club and all of its activities. We now have peace. Eric and Ruby will now have no more worries. We now each go separate ways. We have helped you."

"But what about Jeremy, one of the leaders, he is still free to regroup or more likely escape," replied Roberts.

"He is also dead I am told. His account was closed by one of his customers. The police will probably fill you in if they can catch up with all the previous paperwork," she replied jokingly.

Roberts sighed deeply.

"Why I should run you all in for causing all this mess in the first place, what with foreign agents buying classified information, gunning down private citizens, piracy on the high seas and then there was the dealing in stolen diamonds!"

Tian pretended to be shocked and raised her eyebrows.

"Your citizens are the ones who started all this. They were the thieves . . . traitors. We were only the negotiators for buying what was offered. Then Eric and Ruby were seconded into your pantomime by Roger Davis who was patently underfunded to conduct the minor surveillance operation on two friendly foreign diplomats," she countered.

They all met up outside the house - the agents, the families and two new cigars spirited away in Kasparov's pocket.

Team Leader Roberts had one final thing to say to them all.

"Go home the lot of you. Take up nice hobbies, preferably overseas and don't ever interfere with British Government business ever again . . . oh and I'll see you all in court! You will most likely have to give evidence at the Old Bailey. Now clear off! . . . oh, and thank you!"

Roberts turned to field agent Mary Turner, a.k.a. 'Painter' whispering quietly, "Don't let that one out of your sight Mary. Ruby is Davis's best teen recruit . . . even though she doesn't fully understand that yet . . . or just how good she is."

Roberts and Turner walked towards their vehicles – a Land Rover and a military troop carrier containing the prisoners.

Kasparov looked at Tian thoughtfully.

"Hungry?"

She raised her arm and a shiny dark blue Bentley emerged from the hillside coming towards them. When it came to a stop, the window wound down slowly, exposing an elderly Chinese man with no expression. He looked at a smiling Tian and Kasparov nodding his head slightly. Then he looked over to Ruby.

He beckoned Ruby to the car, held out his hand and gave her a small package the size of a large matchbox. They stared at each other for a moment in mutual understanding.

"This is for you Miss Ruby. Such bravery and honour in a woman so young. Tian and I have much pleasure in recognising your devotion to honour the life of Mister Davis. He would have wanted me to do this I know."

The car moved off slowly as the window closed. The man behind the window now had a soft smile.

Eric watched as Ruby nervously opened the box and let out a combined gasp. Robbie and Harry came over to see why they looked so astonished and excited.

Four glittering, white sparkling diamonds scattered the afternoon sunlight into their eyes.

Harry put his arm around his daughter and kissed her forehead.

"Now you have five diamonds to reckon with."

Kasparov ruffled up Eric's hair as Robbie took a call on his phone.

"Aye yer wee dafties. We'll not be having any use of you all now . . . but I thank you all the same for your support. Eric and Ruby are safe. I'll be seeing you soon at the hotel and it's my shout all round."

Robbie shouted out to Harry, "That was the lads Harry, all ten of them. They had gathered at the hotel to help us out. How am I going to explain all that to Milly?"

They all laughed together. It was all over.

Kasparov raised his arm, looked into the distance whilst shading his eyes and waited.

"What are you doing Ilya? Do you have a car waiting too?" asked Tian.

A shiny black Bentley approached much to everyone's surprise . . . he had commandeered Jeremy's expensive car to take them all back to the Mayfair Mews hotel in Dogbol . . . and Robbie would be driving his new car.

Sir Rodney, Lord Roxburgh and Roland Campignon were taken to the MI6 offices and undertook extensive interrogation before appearing at the Old Bailey. They were duly sentenced to life imprisonment.

Cartwright and Jeremy St John Smythe were dead. Roger Davis and Barrie from MI6, two CIA agents and a boat load of Arab abductors were dead.

Many negotiators had been uncovered by Davis's bogus selling of secrets. Then there were the diamonds.

What price must be paid for such undercover foraging by MI6 to extract the criminals who sell out their country?

My guess is that there is no limit in price or effort. It equally applies to other countries with their own intelligence networks, merely protecting their citizens – who are none the wiser.

Do you think Eric and Ruby had a quiet life? What did they do with the diamonds? Were Tian and Kasparov an item?

I could tell you lots more . . . but that is enough for one day.

Catch up with Ruby in the other books in this trilogy:

Book 2:   **"Diamond for a Ruby"**

Book 3:   **"Ruby's Covert Mission"**

www.ingramcontent.com/pod-product-compliance
Lightning Source LLC
Chambersburg PA
CBHW032001170626
46807CB00006B/2600